WHITE PAWN

VAMPIRE COURT: BOOK 1

Ingrid Seymour

PenDreams • BIRMINGHAM

Published by PenDreams

Cover design by Deranged Doctor Designs

Manufactured in the United States of America
Copyright © 2019 by Ingrid Seymour

ISBN-13: 9781091060333

To Ossie… my feline desk companion

1

I had to admit, he was a handsome thief.

Tall with wavy, brown hair, sun-kissed skin, and mysterious eyes. He moved lithely, his steps and grace as refined as a noble's.

And yet… he was just a thief. Low class, sporting two-day stubble, dressed in battered trousers and coat, his once-white shirt yellowed from use.

I'd spotted him almost as soon as I entered the crowded market street, a city block reserved for brick and mortar stores and makeshift, less permanent stalls.

A shabby leather bag hung across his torso, gently swinging by his side as he strolled from stall to stall, one hand in his pocket, jiggling coins or probably scrap metal of some kind. He wanted to appear as if he had money to purchase goods, but I doubted it.

"What do you think of these, Bianca?" Talyssa, my beloved lady-help, asked from the side.

Her question buzzed in my ear, but I was too intent on the thief to pay her any mind.

"What now?" Talyssa asked in frustration. "Oh, him again?" she added as she spotted the rogue.

Talyssa had been with my family since I was twelve. Papa had brought her from one of the poorer areas of the city to be my companion after Mama died. Talyssa had also lost her mother, and after that, her father hadn't known what to do with her. Pawning her off to a city lord had been an easy way out. He was probably a drunk. I bet he was a drunk. Talyssa never talked about her life with him. It must have been hideous. She'd been fifteen at the time. Now, she was twenty-two and fond of disapproving of everything I did.

"Stop staring at him, Bianca." Talyssa pulled on my arm and forced me to face the stall. "Look at these apples instead." She picked up a bright red piece of fruit and pressed it into my hand.

I rolled my eyes. "Yes, a fine specimen," I said, dropping the apple in Talyssa's basket and glancing over my shoulder, wondering where the thief had gone.

My eyes roved around the different stalls. He wasn't stealing jars of honey or strawberry jam from the old man across from us. He also seemed to have no interest in the potatoes or yams that flooded the burlap sacks in the next stall. He did, however, seem to have a sweet tooth.

I smirked. He had stopped by the baker's kiosk and was eyeing the petite rhubarb tarts. Pointing, he asked something to the baker's assistant, a young boy of around fifteen. The boy held five fingers up, the price of the tarts, which was clearly written on a small sign next to them.

The thief asked for the price of the rolls next, which everyone knew to be one Cheke. The young boy was polite, though, and turned to answer him. While he did so, the thief surreptitiously snatched two tarts and slipped them into his leather bag.

A little gasp escaped me. He'd been so quick, a sleight of hand that had probably taken him years to perfect.

"I was right!" I whispered in Talyssa's ear as she paid the vendor for the apples. "He *is* a thief. He snatched two tarts."

Talyssa whirled and pulled on the sleeve of my red dress. "Hush, Bianca. You don't want to get involved. It's nothing new, goes on every day, I'm sure."

"But the poor assistant," I protested. "He will be in trouble with his master when he doesn't produce the exact amount of money for the goods he was supposed to sell."

"Well," Talyssa said, giving me a raised eyebrow, "if you're so worried about it, why don't *you* pay the boy for the stolen tarts?" She flipped a hand dismissively and moved on to the flower stall.

"That's an idea," I murmured to myself, hurrying toward the baker's kiosk. I pushed past a few ladies and their helpers—my dress rustling as I walked—and caught up with the thief before he moved on to his next target.

"Excuse me," I said, tapping him on the shoulder.

The thief's head snapped back and, for an instant, he looked like he was going to run for his life. When he saw me, however, he seemed to relax.

"Yes, milady?" He smiled and inclined his head.

I was dazzled for a moment. Up close, he was more handsome than I'd realized. His smile was bright, and contrasted perfectly with his golden skin. His eyebrows were thick, black, and glossy. His jaw angular. And his lips… they were full and perfectly shaped.

His dark gaze traveled across my face, assessing me. As he regarded me, his smile deepened.

Something sparked between us. It was unmistakable.

Heat crept slowly up my neck, and in that instant, I was very glad for my tanned skin. It wasn't as deep and rich as the thief's—I didn't spend as much time outside as he probably did—but it did well to cover untimely blushes. Something that made Talyssa very jealous. Her skin was white as porcelain and invariably gave her away when she was embarrassed.

"How… can I help you, milady?" the thief asked once more when I didn't answer, his voice sounded a bit less confident than before, as if he'd also felt the spark.

Straightening to my full height, I took a deep breath and commanded my emotions. This wasn't the first handsome young man I'd ever encountered, and the ones I met at fancy balls every week were much cleaner and better dressed.

"I have a simple request," I said, glad that my tone sounded firmer than his had.

"And what, pray tell, is milady's request?" His voice was steady this time and accompanied by a wink so fast that I almost missed it. I paused, taken aback.

The gall of him!

How dare he wink at me? He was a thief, and I was a lady.

Jutting out my hip, I put out my closed fist. He stared at it and frowned.

"Take this," I ordered, lifting my chin and setting my mouth into a thin line.

My stern posture worked. Immediately, he obeyed me, extending out a hand and placing it underneath mine.

I dropped ten Chekes on his large palm. "Pay the boy for the tarts you *stole*."

For the most part, his face remained steady, but a slight twitch of his eyebrows gave away the fact that I had quite surprised him. He'd thought no one had seen him. He thought he was good at thieving, but I'd just proven otherwise.

His dark eyes dropped to the two black coins in his hand, then returned to my face. He stared into me and held my gaze, saying nothing. I stood my ground, but sitting in the middle of the market, exchanging an intense gaze with a thief was unbecoming of a lady.

"The boy is likely an apprentice, *thief*," I said because the silence got the best of me. "And when he gets back, he'll have to explain to his master why he's short on change. It will, without a doubt, cost him his post, his livelihood."

He narrowed his eyes at me. "And *you* care about that?"

I narrowed my eyes back. I wasn't stupid. This was a trick question. If I said I cared, he would condemn me for being better off than the boy. And if I said I didn't care, he would probably smirk.

"I care not to have *thieves* wandering about Acedrex, *my city*. And I'm sure the White Queen and Black King don't either," I said.

Since no one dared defy the two powerful vampires, Acedrex's monarchs kept the city safe and in immaculate order. In spite of the most unsavory aspects of their rule, we had peace—unlike other neighboring lands.

This market was on a white square of the city, therefore ruled by Queen Lovina and kept safe by her Sentries. The entire city was divided into sixty-four alternating black or white sections, like a chessboard, like the silly game our whole existence was modeled after. White sections were controlled by the Queen, and black ones by the King.

It had been so since the original vampire Queen and King had replaced human monarchs centuries ago. History taught us that there had been tremendous hate between them but, unable to defeat each other due to their perfectly matched strengths, they had played a game of chess to decide the best way to rule Acedrex, thus affecting the fate of generations to come.

The thief snorted. "If you're worried about thieves, you should probably hold on tighter to your Chekes," he said, pocketing the coins I'd given him.

I gasped. "You can't do that."

"Oh, dear!" Talyssa came running and immediately started pulling me away from the thief. "Get away from that person."

The shoppers around us went quiet and turned curious stares in our direction, but I didn't care. I would not let this thief take advantage of me.

Determined to unmask him once and for all, I yanked my arm out of Talyssa's grip and, in my blind haste, knocked the shopping basket out of her grip, sending the fruits and purple dahlias crashing to the ground.

"Oh, gods!" she exclaimed, watching the apples roll all around her as her cheeks reddened. She leaned down and picked up the flowers, looking quite distraught.

"Oh my, this is terrible," the thief said, snatching Talyssa's basket off the ground. "Let me help."

Before I managed to get my wits back, the thief picked up all the apples, returned them to the basket, and handed them back to Talyssa.

"Here you go, milady," he said with a brilliant smile.

"Oh," Talyssa pressed a hand to her bosom, a blush climbing from her chest all the way up to her face, making her redder still. "Thank you." She batted her eyelashes.

Oh, please. I rolled my eyes. This was too much.

"Sentries!" I screamed.

The thief sighed. "You didn't have to do that."

I gave him a raised eyebrow.

"Sentries, a thief," I screamed even louder this time.

"If we meet again," he said, placing a hand on his heart and bowing, "I would like you to know and remember my name is Nyro."

Hurried steps sounded behind the stalls. The Sentries were coming. I turned toward the sound of their heavy boots as they smacked the cobblestone street.

"This way!" I called.

Two men and a woman dressed in white uniforms appeared around one of the stalls. Their coats had black accents around the neck and wrists, as well as black belts around the waist. They belonged to the White Queen's ranks.

"Catch that thief," I said, pointing toward the shameless individual.

The Sentries blinked and stared at me with matching frowns.

"Well, don't just stand there. Catch him." I swiveled.

The thief was gone.

Spinning in a circle, I searched for him among the shoppers and stalls. He was nowhere to be found.

"He… he was just right there," I said, feeling stupid. "He stole from me and the baker's boy."

"What? Me?!" said the baker boy, who had stepped away from his stall to gawk. He turned back to his goods and frantically started counting them.

I shook my head. "I'm such an idiot," I mumbled.

"Bianca," Talyssa said, sidling up to me, "maybe we should get back home. It does no good for a lady to be involved in these kinds of things."

"But he—"

"Let's go." She unceremoniously took my hand and started pulling me in the direction of home.

Anger made itself comfortable in the pit of my stomach. I hated to lose, but there was nothing to be done.

"Fine," I said, yanking my hand from Talyssa's death grip and stomping like a petulant child.

If I ever see him again…

I didn't know what I would do to him, but he would pay for embarrassing me this way.

Fifteen minutes later—after a brisk walk one square south and two squares west, out of the market and past many houses—we reached home.

It was located on Square B2, a black section on the chessboard that was our city.

Going past the low stone wall that surrounded Flagfall House, I walked down the path that led to the front steps. The marigolds Talyssa and I had planted a few weeks ago flanked me on both sides, lifting my spirits slightly.

A short set of steps led to the carved stone doorway of my two-story house. Symmetrical windows sat under a pitched roof, and perfectly trimmed hedges surrounded the perimeter.

Talyssa kept pace behind me, holding up her dress. "It's ridiculous letting a thief get you this upset," she continued in the monologue she'd started when we left the market.

I ignored her and pushed the door open, leaving the sunny summer morning behind. I took off my lace gloves and discarded them on the entryway console, where the flower vase stood empty. I had accompanied Talyssa to the market to purchase fresh flowers for the foyer, and now they were trampled.

My day was quite ruined, and I thought it couldn't get any worse.

Except I turned out to be wrong, because as I marched into the library—wishing to tell Papa what had happened—my day got far, far worse.

A tall, thick man was standing in our library, towering over my father in a threatening way. He was dressed in a black suit with a matching bowler hat, his pale face contrasting with his dark garments. He turned my way as I entered the room, allowing me a better look.

At the sight of his pallid skin, I gasped. Talyssa came to a stop behind me and let out a small shriek.

This was no ordinary man.

It was a Black Rook.

One of his meaty hands was on Papa's shoulders, squeezing, blue-green veins cording the skin. I knew he was a Rook because he wore an insignia on the right shoulder of his jacket, the unmistakable white outline of a castle turret.

My heart hammered for Papa's safety. Rooks were the Queen and King's thugs. They did their dirty work. What could one of them possibly want with my father? As Flagfall House was located on a black square, it was controlled by the Black King, but never had one of his Board set foot here.

Through the knot that had immediately formed in my throat, I managed to ask, "Papa, is something the matter?"

He shook his head ever so slightly, putting on a forced smile. "It's nothing, dear. Please go to your room."

I wanted to protest, but I was afraid to cause trouble for Papa, so I slowly started to back out of the room.

The Rook narrowed his eyes, his nose twitching as if he smelled something in the air.

"Stop!" he ordered me.

"She's just a bothersome girl, Rook Datcu," Papa said in a dismissive tone. "Let us finish discussing our business."

"Quiet," Rook Datcu said, holding up a thick finger.

Then, without taking his eyes off me, he stalked in my direction. I stood completely frozen, while Talyssa whimpered behind me.

2

Rook Datcu took three long strides and stopped a mere foot away from me. Talyssa's hand slipped into mine, giving me strength and support. Even so, my knees trembled at the sight of the Rook's ivory-white face and red-rimmed eyes. This man—no, this creature, like other Board members of high rank—had consumed the King's blood and gained an appetite for more.

Was he thinking of consuming mine?

Papa clumsily rushed in my direction, ready to make an appeal on my behalf. Without even turning, Rook Datcu held a hand up and spoke in a growl.

"Stay," he said, as if he were dealing with a dog and not a respected member of the city.

Like a dog, Papa obeyed, his gray eyes darting back and forth in fear.

Rook Datcu leaned closer, his nose twitching, lowering toward my neck. A chill went down my spine as I stared into his unnatural eyes. They must have once been blue since I could see splashes of that color in their depths. Now, however, they were mostly of a muddy brown, like dried blood, like death.

I inclined my head back, trying to keep the distance between us. But he continued to move closer, finally forcing me to take a step backward.

His chest rumbled in anger. He clutched my wrist with bruising force, yanking me forward. I yelped as my breasts collided with his chest. Talyssa squeezed my hand harder.

"Please, don't hurt her," Papa said. "I'll pay everything I owe."

Pay?

But I barely had time to linger on that thought before the Rook pressed his nose to the base of my neck and inhaled deeply, making a shuddering sound.

I wanted to flee, to turn into a bug and crawl under the rug, to disappear. This beast was sniffing me, his free hand wrapped around my waist, his mouth moving against my collarbone.

Did he have fangs? I knew he wasn't a vampire—not yet, probably not ever, since the Black King had been in rule for so long and no challenger had ever defeated him—but he *did* drink blood. That was common knowledge. Bishops, Knights and Rooks took a taste of their monarch's blood before assuming their posts, and after that, they craved its taste. Only Pawns were exempt from the horrible deed—not that they could be trusted.

Trembling, I waited for the Rook to bite me. He trembled as well.

After an eternity, he slowly pulled away, as if it pained him. He let go of me, his mouth twisted in a sneer.

Turning to Papa, he asked, "What do we have here?"

Papa shook his head, glancing at me, his expression darkening with a mixture of guilt, shame, and fear. What had happened? And why did I suddenly feel as if Papa had just condemned me to death?

℘ ℭ

Papa was pacing in front of the sofa and had been for the past fifteen minutes. I sat on a chair, watching him go back and forth, waiting for an answer he seemed incapable of giving me.

Rook Datcu was outside the closed door, making sure we didn't go anywhere. He had ordered a bewildered Talyssa to fetch ink and paper and, after writing a hasty letter, had sent our footman on errand to King Maximus's palace.

Talyssa sat on an upholstered chair, one knee bouncing up and down, hands twisting on her lap. Her nose was red from crying, but the rest of her face was white as a sheet.

"Papa," I begged again, "please tell me what is happening."

Still pacing, he grabbed his head as if he feared it might fall off his shoulders. For a moment, I thought he would go on without speaking, but he suddenly asked the most nonsensical question possible.

"Did you drink your tea this morning?"

I frowned. "What?"

"Talyssa," he turned to my lady-help. "Did she drink her tea?

"I took it to her room, my Lord," Talyssa said, confused.

"But did she drink it?" Papa pressed.

Talyssa glanced at me, then gave a small shrug.

"What does that have to do with anything?" I demanded.

"It's got everything to do with EVERYTHING!" he exclaimed, startling me. Papa never raised his voice. Never.

Stupidly, tears gathered in my eyes. I pulled my handkerchief from under my sleeve and dabbed at my eyes.

"I'm sorry, Bianca," Papa said, kneeling in front of me and taking my hand in his. "This is not your fault. Oh, child." His eyes wavered. He lowered his head. There was that shame again. Why?

"If your mother were still alive, she would hate me," he said, still avoiding my gaze.

"You're scaring me, Papa," I said in a whisper. "Please, tell me, why did the Rook summon King Maximus to our house?"

Why had the Rook come to our house in the first place? Not even a Black Sentry had ever crossed our threshold. How had we gone from that to this? Catching the King or Queen's attention was not good. They were vampires. They left their human subjects alone for the most part, but they didn't tolerate those who caused unrest or went against their rule in any way.

Papa shook himself and pulled up a chair. Sitting in front of me, he inhaled deeply and asked about my morning tea again.

"Did you drink your tea?"

I wanted to scream and tell him I didn't care about the stupid tea, but it had to be important for him to mention it again.

"I don't remember," I said. "Talyssa brought it to my room while I was changing, and I was distracted by a stubborn curl that didn't want to comply." I touched the side of my head, recalling my frustration. "So I set the tea down, and… I guess I forgot to drink it."

Papa pressed a hand to his mouth, his expression twisting in despair.

"Dear gods," he murmured behind the cage of his fingers.

Mind swirling as if a storm had been unleashed within me, I said, "You told me the tea was to keep me healthy, but that isn't true, is it?" I asked, fearing the worst.

Papa shook his head.

"What is it for then?" I asked, terribly afraid of the answer.

"The tea is from bloodshade leaves," he said, his hands trembling as he twisted them together.

My heart froze. I slowly shook my head as if in a dream. Talyssa gasped.

"Your mother used to drink it, too. Every day." Papa's eyes became unfocused, as if lost in a memory of Mama holding a teacup and smiling.

My insides constricted as if Talyssa were pulling violently on my corset, the way she tended to do when she was cross with me. A tear slid down my cheek as I pictured Mama drinking the bloodshade.

"It can't be," I said in a whisper. "I'm not a…" I couldn't finish.

But Papa finished for me.

"You are a *Trove*, Bianca."

15

෨ ൚

A Trove.

My lips trembled. That was impossible. It couldn't be. I shook my head in denial.

"No. No. How can you know such a thing, Papa? You must be mistaken. Troves are rare. And... and only King Maximus and Queen Lovina would be able to tell. If I were a Trove, they would have found me already, and I would live in one of the palaces."

I laughed at the ludicrous suggestion, my insides quivering as I did so. The thought of living at the White or Black Palace sawed fear deep in my soul.

From what I knew, the blood of a Trove was delicious to vampires. But not only that, the blood gave them energy for days. One feeding, and the King and Queen of Acedrex could even withstand sunlight.

Papa lowered his head. "They have found you now. He smelled it on you, even though yesterday's bloodshade must still be in your system. Rooks are trained to do that," Papa said, gesturing toward the door, then glancing toward Talyssa in a strange way, as if she blamed her for what had happened. "Oh, how your mother and I prayed you had not inherited the trait from her, but..."

"No!" I stood and stomped to the fireplace. "It must be something else. I'm not... one of those *things*, and Mama wasn't either."

If it was true, King Maximus would take me, and I would be his slave to the end of my days.

I whirled and faced Papa. "Why was that Rook here in the first place?" I demanded.

Papa shook his head and looked away. "That doesn't matter now."

I rushed to his side and pulled him to his feet. "That must be the reason why Rook Datcu sent for the King. It has nothing to do with me."

Papa regarded me with wet eyes, his expression telling me he wished that were true.

"No, dear. The King does not involve himself with gamblers," he said, shutting his eyes and causing a tear to drop and cut a line down his cheek.

"Gamblers?" I repeated numbly.

Papa turned his back on me, hiding his face. Talyssa pressed a hand to her mouth.

"You've been gambling?" I asked.

His shoulders stiffened, and it was all I needed for an answer.

"Oh, Papa. How could you?" My throat seemed to close, and the words came out in gasps.

He had always criticized gamblers, those careless men who endangered their lives attending the chess dens, men who bet their money, and sometimes even their blood, in hopes of doubling their fortune. But why would he resort to such a thing? We had no need for it. The inheritance Mama had left behind was large enough for Papa and I to live comfortably for the rest of our lives— even enough for me to attract a respectable husband.

"Why?" I asked, desperate to understand. "Were you *that* bored?"

"I… I've made some mistakes," he said, walking away, his back still to me. "Some of my investments didn't go as planned."

"What investments? We have no need for investments. Mama left us—"

"I thought I could increase our fortune," he continued, as if I hadn't spoken. "So we could leave this godsforsaken place, so we could get away from this vampire court. I've always worried about you. I didn't want you to be discovered."

"But Papa, no one ever leaves Acedrex," I said between clenched teeth. Not without permission from the Queen or King themselves.

"A bribe large enough can do it," he said.

"So you did the one thing that would bring a Rook into our home?" I asked in a shrill voice that made my face grow warm with shame. Papa and I had always had a relationship based on respect. We'd never raised our voices to each other before, but today seemed to have destroyed all those rules.

He finally faced me and, with obvious difficulty, met my gaze. "I lost everything," he said, nearly shaking. "I thought I could salvage the situation, so I gambled what little was left. But I've lost even that."

I raised a trembling hand to my chest. "Are you saying… we're poor?"

Papa collapsed on a chair, burying his face in his liver-spotted hands.

Feeling disoriented, I glanced around the library: the books on the shelves, Mama's small paintings on the wall, the rugs covering the polished, wooden floor…

I lost everything, Papa's words echoed in my mind.

Did that mean he'd lost the house, too?

I'd just opened my mouth to ask when the sound of an approaching carriage sent my heart pattering. Papa jumped to his feet and stepped in front of me protectively. But what was the use? He had failed to keep me safe the moment he allowed greed to enter his heart.

I exchanged a fearful glance with Talyssa, who still had a hand pressed to her mouth.

King Maximus was here. The Vampire King in my mother's house, here to taste my blood and discover whether or not I was a Trove.

My hands trembled. I twisted my lace handkerchief between my fingers. If I was a Trove, it wouldn't matter that Papa had squandered our money. I would go to court, and I would lack for nothing... except I would always be a slave, a blood vessel for the King's enjoyment. The Trove curse ran in families, but it could skip entire generations and never appear again. Vampires had tried breeding Troves for centuries to their utter frustration. By some unknown mercy, once a vampire fed from a Trove, it seemed that person became incapable of bearing offspring with the trait. So as the King's slave, I would never marry or have children.

I would be *owned*.

And if I wasn't a Trove, what would be my fate? Would I have to become a beggar on the streets?

Dear gods. I didn't want to be either.

3

Papa and I stood frozen, intent on the sounds outside the door. Heavy steps sounded against the wooden floor, followed by deep silence. Talyssa jumped to her feet and joined me, taking hold of my hand.

My heart raced while I fought to breathe normally. I had never seen King Maximus, not even from a distance. When he drank from a Trove, he was perfectly safe to be out in the daylight, but rumor had it he despised sunlight and much preferred the night. Quite the opposite of the White Queen, who I had seen surveying the populace from her royal carriage more times than I cared to count.

There was a likeness of King Maximus at the Central Acedrex Museum, one Talyssa and I had seen on our first visit there when I was thirteen. We'd held hands in front of the portrait, trembling inside our hooped dresses, spellbound by the King's strange eyes. It seemed ludicrous to be so spooked by a mere portrait, but after we left, we'd comforted each other by reassuring ourselves we would never have to meet him.

And now...

I waited to hear the King's voice or at least Rook Datcu's, but there was only silence. Then the door opened and time seemed to stand still as the King of Acedrex, the vampire who had ruled the Black Court for the last two hundred and seventy-five years walked through the door.

The air around me chilled as if summer had suddenly turned to bitter winter. Papa took a step back, pushing us toward the wall as King Maximus glided into the room, the sound of his boots striking the floor utterly incongruous.

He was dressed all in black, including the shirt under his tight vest. A top hat rested on his head. White blond hair peeked from under the hat, almost matching the ghostly white of his skin. His eyes shone dark red, like spilled blood on a butcher's block. He carried an ebony walking stick that stood in stark contrast against his pale hand.

Black and white like a chessboard.

The only splash of color on his garments was a slender red ribbon worn around his neck in place of a tie or kerchief. Its ends fell lazily over his chest, making me think of two thin streams of blood dripping from his fangs.

Blue-green veins rose from his collar, up the column of his tall neck and over his jaw. But, even as beastly as he appeared, he was still handsome and alluring: a tempting predator with the appeal of a carnivorous flower.

The door to the library shut, leaving us alone with the creature. Legend had it that centuries ago, before Acedrex was ruled by vampires, they were unable to go inside people's homes unless they were invited. If that were ever true, something had clearly changed since then because he was now easily strolling into our house, even though we didn't want him here.

He came to a stop at the edge of the rug as if it were a boundary of some kind.

With utmost grace, the King removed his hat, tucked it under his arm, and stared at us from head to toe.

"My King." Papa hurried to bow, looking as submissive as possible.

King Maximus ignored him, his crimson eyes moving lazily from Talyssa to me. Nose twitching like a dog's, he leaned forward ever so slightly and inhaled. After pondering for a moment, he frowned, appearing confused.

"You," he said, his gaze finally going to Papa, "have been hiding a Trove from me." The King's voice was low, like the rumble of stones. There was no question in his tone. Instead, an accusation and a threat, all in one.

I stepped next to Papa and slipped my hand into his.

He had smelled me and had determined I was, indeed, a Trove.

My teeth chattered as if I were naked in the middle of a winter storm. I was to be a slave. A swoon came over me, but I clenched my fists and, drawing strength from Papa's warmth, managed to stay on my feet. I would not let this beast break me with its inhumane stare.

He could take me, but I would find an escape. Then, I would come back for Papa, and we would run far, far away from here. I wouldn't be anyone's property.

I was Bianca Flagfall, and I would stand my ground as always.

In my mind, I saw my escape play out. It wouldn't be easy once I managed to slip out of King Maximus's castle, but Papa and I would find a way. As long as I had him, being a beggar would be better than being a slave.

But what my mind had so naively conjured was not to be.

Not after Papa took a trembling Talyssa by the arm and pushed her in front of the King. Papa glowered at my childhood friend and companion with rage and hatred, two things I had never seen in his gentle eyes.

"Is that what you are?" he demanded. "How could you trick us this way?"

§ ☙

Talyssa staggered forward, letting out a shrill squeak. She looked left and right as if searching for an escape route. Then, she peered back at Papa, her eyes as wide as saucers. Her expression was pleading and seemed to ask, *Why are you doing this?*

A gasp caught in my throat. What did Papa intend? This would not trick the King. All he'd have to do was smell Talyssa, and he would know it was a desperate lie.

I wanted to step forward and protect my friend, but I found that my limbs were locked. Shock paralyzed me, the fear coursing through my veins too great to overcome.

King Maximus gently set his hat and walking cane on top of a chair and stepped into the square of the rug. His beastly eyes were set on Talyssa as his nostrils widened, and his red tongue licked the corner of his pale mouth.

Talyssa whimpered as the vampire approached.

I let go of Papa's hand and stepped forward. "Don't hurt her," I said.

But it was in vain because, in a blur faster than my eyes could see, the King burrowed his face into Talyssa's neck and pulled her tight against him. At the same time, Papa wrapped an arm around my waist and pulled me back, attempting to turn me away from the horror, but I was transfixed. As Papa shoved me face first against the wall, my head swiveled, eyes locked on the mesmerizing horror.

"Talyssa," I said in a whisper, my hand reaching out in her direction.

Her shape was bent backwards as the vampire curved into her, drinking her blood. Her hands dangled at her side as she let out a moan of… pleasure. My stomach twisted at the sound.

Was she enjoying it? The creature's hungry mouth against the tender flesh of her neck? The sapping of her life?

His… *feeding* seemed to go on forever, but in truth, it only lasted a few seconds.

Holding my friend as a child would a doll, King Maximus deposited Talyssa's limp body on the chaise lounge. She sank lifelessly into it, one of her arms falling to the side, her head hanging. Two red puncture marks marred the creamy skin of her neck.

Tears spilled from my eyes uncontrollably. Was she dead? Had he murdered her? Ended her precious life in seconds as if she were nothing but a bug under a heavy boot?

Talyssa let out a tiny moan. My heart lifted. She was alive! Relief filled me until the King's quiet purr filled me with dread again.

"Not a particularly powerful Trove, but a Trove after all," he said in his ancient, rumbling voice.

A tiny drop of crimson stained his lower lip. Like a snake's, his tongue darted out and licked it off, making my insides shiver. Smoothly, he pulled out a black handkerchief from his breast pocket and dabbed his mouth with it.

"Now, you." King Maximus's eyes snapped back to Papa.

I almost screamed at the sight of his vivid red gaze. His eyes were swimming with my friend's blood, and the veins that rose from his neck were slowly disappearing, receding under his shirt's collar as if someone were pulling them downward.

"No one *steals* from me," he said to Papa.

"I… I didn't know, my King. I swear," Papa said.

I knew Papa well, and in his voice, I heard the lie. He'd known Talyssa was a Trove. But if he had, why hadn't he also insisted that she drank the bloodshade tea?

The answer, ugly and gnarled, promptly revealed itself to me.

Papa had brought Talyssa into our home for more than one reason. Besides being lady-help, my companion, she was always meant to be a decoy if something like this ever happened.

I tried to push the realization away. Papa wasn't capable of such coldness. He couldn't be.

"You're a terrible liar," King Maximus said.

Stuttering, Papa began to protest, but the King's voice rose above his.

"No one *steals* from me," he repeated. "No one *lies* to me. No one who lives to tell the tale, anyway."

King Maximus lifted a hand. Black, curved claws sprang from the tips of his fingers. I sprang forward to pull Papa back, but I wasn't fast enough. The King brought his hand down, swiping across Papa's abdomen with vicious speed and force.

Like knives, the vampire's claws cut into him, sending blood flying into my face. A cry of pain tore from Papa's throat.

Blinded, I crashed against him as he started to fall. We toppled, falling backward. Desperately, I swatted at my eyes with my sleeve. Through crimson tears, I saw Papa's grimace of pain.

The wound in his stomach bubbled with blood. I pressed a hand to it, trying to stanch its flow.

"Papa, Papa," I cried.

King Maximus stood above, staring at us with an expression of disgust as he wiped his killing hand with the same black handkerchief he'd used for his mouth.

"The stench," he said, taking a step back, his expression twisting further. "Datcu," he called without raising his voice.

The Rook opened the door and stepped into the room.

"Your Majesty?" he said, inclining his head.

"The Trove," he pointed at Talyssa's immobile shape on the chaise lounge, "take her to the palace and put her with the others."

Rook Datcu frowned, his gaze going from Talyssa to me. He had smelled me, but Talyssa had been standing next to me. I could almost see the cogwheels working in his mind and resolving that he'd made a mistake, for how could his King be fooled?

How, indeed?

I pressed my forehead to Papa's shoulder and wept.

The bloodshade must still be working on you, Papa had said.

"These two," King Maximus pointed in our direction next, "leave them here. The *thief* will suffer for a bit longer. The girl... she's innocent, I suppose. Let her live."

Discarding his black kerchief, the King turned on his heel and walked out. The echoes of his words played in my ears as Rook Datcu picked Talyssa up and carried her away with him, while the blood-stained piece of silk the King had used to clean himself floated to the floor, the falling flag that signaled our doom.

4

A wet cough racked Papa's weakening body.

"Help! Help us!" I yelled, using the skirts of my dress to try to stop the flow of blood.

No one came. No one lived near enough to hear my cries, and the servants had surely fled out the back door the moment they realized what was happening.

Papa coughed again as he tried to say something.

"Don't talk please," I begged, watching his paling face through a curtain of tears.

"Take… the… bloodshade and leave," he said in a hoarse voice. "Go far away… from this house."

I shook my head. "We'll go together. We'll figure out a way to leave Acedrex and find a nice place to live and—"

"There's… money in the desk in my room. Ta-take that, too." He coughed violently, speckles of blood spraying the air.

"Papa, Papa…" I said between sobs.

"Forgive m-me," he said, then let out a drawn out breath and went still.

"No." I shook him, stared into his ghostly face. "Papa, don't leave me."

I pressed my face to his chest and cried, begging him not to go.

I don't know how long I stayed that way, but when I finally tried to stand, my legs would not respond. Crawling on hands and knees, I reached a chair and used it to help me to my feet. Two bloody handprints stained the seat once I pulled away. I stared at the blemishes with detachment.

This morning, a minor blot on the rug would have sent me running into the kitchen in search of a clean cloth and vinegar, but now that the entire world had collapsed around me, what did it matter?

This morning, a life full of promise and happiness had laid before me, and now, there was nothing.

In a trance, I wandered through the house, running my bloodied fingers along the wall and every piece of furniture in my path.

Subconsciously following Papa's instructions, I made it to the kitchen and approached the cupboard where Louisa, the cook, kept my morning tea. I opened a drawer and pulled out a small box that rested easily in the palms of my hands. A familiar, bitter aroma rose from it. Talyssa hated the smell, but I'd always liked it.

Carrying the box, I went into Papa's bedroom. The scents here were familiar too, and it was almost impossible to walk across the room to his desk without collapsing on his bed, crying.

A pouch full of Chekes rested in the bottom of one of the drawers. A small dagger also occupied the space. Ignoring the money, I picked up the weapon and gripped it tightly.

King Maximus's evil face flashed before my eyes, and I imagined the dagger cutting across his throat, the way his claws had cut Papa's stomach. Even so, I knew a wound like that couldn't kill him. I could cut him a thousand times, dismember him limb by limb, and he would still live.

There was only one way to kill a vampire, and I was too weak to do it.

You could change that, a voice whispered inside my head. *You could become strong and take away everything he holds dear, just like he did you.*

I nodded to myself, an intense emotion filling my chest. I'd never felt anything so completely, never seen a goal so clearly.

It would not be easy, and I would probably die trying, but what was the alternative? Flee and die anyway? I wouldn't make it alone. I had no relatives. I didn't know anyone who would take pity on me—not that I wanted anyone's pity and charity.

I lowered the dagger, holding it so tightly that my knuckles turned white.

"Wait for me Talyssa," I murmured. "Be strong, for no matter how long it takes me, I will come for you."

5

After cleaning myself, I changed into a simple skirt and blouse and packed a small suitcase with similar garments. No hoops, no lace, no bonnets, just the kind of clothes I normally wore on lazy days.

Removing the dry bloodshade leaves from the box, I stuffed a few into my mouth, then transferred them to a bag with a drawstring and hid them in the case between my clothes. The dagger and money, I kept on myself, hidden at my waist, under my skirt.

I would have to figure out where to acquire more bloodshade, but that was a problem for another day. At the moment, I had enough to last me a month, perhaps more.

My plan wasn't the best, considering what I was: a Trove. But Papa had often accused me of being an insensible girl, and without him here, I saw no point in changing my ways.

Suitcase in hand, I left my bedroom and walked out of the house without looking back. Papa wasn't there anymore. His spirit had left this world, and there was no reason to mourn the shell that was left behind.

I had no doubt that King Maximus's Rooks would soon take possession of what had always been the King's property. Flagfall House was built on a black square, after all.

But Acedrex wasn't entirely his. He shared the privilege of ownership with someone else.

The Queen Lovina, and it was to her palace where I was headed.

೮ ೧೪

It seemed ridiculous to think that a game of chess had, thousands of years ago, decided Acedrex's fate. But all one had to do was look around to see it was true.

We lived on a chessboard, ruled by a White Queen and a Black King. Bullied by their Rooks, and "protected" by their Knights, Pawns, and Sentries. Our monarchs' Boards.

Once, a millennia ago, vampires had infested this land. There had been so many of them that they'd nearly wiped out the entire human population, feeding on them at leisure, making game of hunting and killing them.

Two vampires, a male and a female, both smarter and more powerful than the others, saw their food supply quickly dwindling and decided to do something about it. Ruthlessly, they set out to annihilate their brethren, until they were the only two vampires left.

In their greed, they sought to destroy each other, too, for how could there be trust between them after what they'd done?

Their fight went on for years until, tired of constantly watching their backs, they agreed to settle the score over a game of chess.

The female vampire won, and with strange, ironic wisdom set out to base their form of government on the game of chess itself. So she had created a White and a Black Court and divided the city into perfect squares.

She became the White Queen and he, the Black King. They built the city, and a tall, thick wall around it. Inside, on the East and West ends, atop two hills, they erected separate palaces and filled them with human servants and others to help govern the city, which they named Acedrex, in honor of the game.

Two Bishops, two Rooks, two Knights and eight Pawns filled their Board, their governing body, while Sentries comprised their guard.

Fearing boredom in her eternal life, the Queen ensured her amusement by leaving a door open for a line of succession, a way for even a mere Pawn to be promoted to Queen or King. She didn't make it easy, but it wasn't impossible.

Now, the original Queen and King were dead and had been so for millennia. Through the centuries, other queens and kings had come and gone. They'd joined the White and Black Boards as Pawns, had fought their way up the ranks until they became Bishops, and earned their right to challenge and kill their monarchs to become full-fledged vampires and rulers of Acedrex.

And it was this very thing that I, Bianca Flagfall, intended to do.

King Maximus would die. I would become the White Queen, a vampire.

And I would kill him.

℘ ℭ

By the time I arrived at the gates of the White Palace, night had fallen.

Flickering lights shone from the windows of the manors that flanked the palace: the homes of the nobles who lived in utter privilege and comfort and outside the boundaries of the chessboard. Papa and I had lived well, but our fortune had been nothing compared to theirs. I'd aspired to become the wife of one of the men who lived in those manors, but that goal now seemed empty compared to my new one.

I should have been nervous walking up the steep road that led to the White Palace, but I was not. The type of fear I had known this morning meant nothing now. Thieves and bandits seemed harmless compared to what I'd already been through.

The Queen's lair stood prominently atop a big hill, its spires peeking past the tall wall that surrounded it. I had never been inside or seen more than its white, conical tops. Tonight, that would change.

I came to a stop in front of the gates, set my suitcase down and faced the two Sentries, a man and a woman, who walked up to meet me. Their ivory uniforms stood out against the night as they eyed me up and down as if I were an apparition. Swords hung from their belts, while two torches burned on each side of the gate, casting swaying shadows around us.

"Ma'am," the woman said, "petitions are only accepted the first Monday of each month and *in the morning.*"

"I'm not here to petition anything," I said, trying not to squirm under their roving gazes.

"Then why are you here?" the male Sentry asked, stroking his black beard and lifting an eyebrow. He was broad and a full head taller than me.

That's when I noticed the Pawn-shaped insignias sewn to the right sleeve of their uniforms. My heart drummed, and sweat trickled down my back. These guards were not simple Sentries, they were Pawns, members of the Queen's Board.

Calm down, Bianca, I told myself. *They're just Pawns who, most likely, will never make it to the next rank.*

"Maybe you meant to go to the Black Palace instead," the male Pawn said. "King Maximus enjoys the odd human girl once and again."

They chuckled at the crude joke.

Tears prickled the back of my eyes. I had never been so disrespected in my life. Still, I swallowed the lump that threatened to form in my throat and stood straighter, reaching my full height.

"No," I said. "I'm just where I intend to be."

Which meant I'd gone as far away from King Maximus as I could: the White Court.

"Is that so?" the bearded Pawn asked, regarding me curiously.

I imagined myself turning and running down the hill away from this place and its awful possibilities, but the moment of cowardice passed, and I remained firm.

"That is so," I said. "I call upon my right to join the Board."

The Pawns exchanged puzzled glances.

"You?" the male Pawn asked, his accent changing from formal to that of a commoner. "You don't look like the type." His expression softened somewhat, and he added, "the Board ain't no place for someone like you, little lady. You'd be better off finding a courtly husband, one of those well-dressed dandies who love attending balls. Don't yeh think, Vinna?"

"I'd have to agree, Alben," Vinna said, rubbing her cropped hair, which looked coppery under the light from the torches. Her accent was also that of a commoner.

"You have no right to refuse me," I said firmly. "I know the law."

"Refuse yeh?" Vinna backed away, her hands up in the air. "Ain't no one said anything 'bout refusing you. Just trying to offer some friendly advice."

"Yeah," Alben added. "You'll get us in trouble if you go 'round saying we refused yeh."

"I'm sorry," I said. "I'm not trying to get anyone in trouble. It's just…" Tears came to my eyes, and my voice threatened to break, but I managed to finish. "My father died tonight, and I have nowhere else to go."

Vinna stuffed her hands in her pockets, looking chagrined. Alben shuffled from foot to foot, his attention suddenly drawn to the ground.

"Um, I'm sorry, little lady," Alben said after a stretch of uncomfortable silence. "We meant no disrespect. Vinna, why don't yeh take her inside, let her talk to Knight Kelsus? Send a Sentry to replace yeh."

Vinna nodded and extended her hand toward a side door. She let me walk ahead of her until we got inside. From there, she led me to the left down a long, covered corridor that ran along the outer stone wall. To the right, the corridor was open, facing a grand courtyard and past that, a long grassy field that extended toward the majestic palace in the distance.

"Sorry about yer pa," Vinna said. "I lost mine when I was seven. Ma couldn't feed three mouths on her own, so soon as I turned sixteen—that was two year ago—she sent me here to join the Board. I send them half my salary. So I guess I'm also here because my pa died."

I nodded, unsure of what to say.

"Sorry if Alben and I were rude at first," she said as the corridor ended, and we walked through a door into a small building. "We get lots of fools at the gates who don't know what's good for them."

"I understand," I said. "No need to apologize."

The room we walked into was ample and furnished with several long tables and wooden benches at each side. It appeared to be some sort of dining hall. We moved slowly between the rows as Vinna let me take in the few additional details, such as the swords hanging from the stone walls, and the large coat of arms set proudly above the door toward which we were headed. The heraldic emblem consisted of a shield with a crown on top, a chessboard pattern in the center, and a metal plate with the words "Semper Lumen" carved in it.

Always Light.

The coat of arms was as familiar to me as that of the Black Court, which was exactly the same as this one, except with the words "Semper Tenebris" carved into it. The shields were a common sight all over Acedrex, a constant reminder of our rulers. As if we could ever forget.

"Knight Kelsus is probably still in his office," Vinna said, stopping in front of the wide door, knocking, and lowering her voice to say, "You're lucky me and

Alben were the ones on duty. Knight Kelsus is a decent man. We're in his Quadrant."

A decent man? Was that possible in this place? Could he even be considered a *man* after drinking the Queen's blood?

"Come in," a voice said from within.

Vinna pushed the door open and walked in.

Knight Kelsus was sitting behind a large desk, writing intently, an inkwell to his right. A similar desk sat empty next to his. I assumed it belonged to the Queen's second Knight.

"What is it?" he asked, without lifting his eyes from the page.

"Knight Kelsus, I bring you a new Challenger."

 ℘ ℮

Knight Kelsus stopped writing and lifted dark brown eyes flecked with red in my direction. I expected him to show surprise when he saw me, but his expression was unreadable.

Setting his quill down, he stood and came to stand in front of the desk. He was tall and imposing in his white uniform, which contrasted beautifully against his dark skin. His hair was shoulder-length and was twisted in many small sections in the fashion of the island folk who were often seen trading in the markets. Outsiders weren't normally allowed to become Acedrex's citizens, so there must have been an interesting story behind his admittance and, furthermore, an even more interesting one to explain how he was now a member of the White Board.

"Please, come in Ms…" he let the word hang.

I hadn't realized I was still standing outside the door. My stomach flipped with nerves. Once I crossed the threshold, there would be no turning back. Was I really ready? What if they tested me somehow to see if I was a Trove? Had I been too hasty in my decision?

After searching myself for a moment, I found I still felt the same way I had when I left home.

I wanted vengeance.

"Ms. Bianca Flagfall," I said, entering the room.

"A pleasure, Ms. Flagfall," Knight Kelsus said, displaying a perfect, white smile. "Vinna, you may leave."

"Yes, Knight." She saluted, extending her arm out, forming a forty-five degree angle with the floor. Then she left, closing the door and leaving me alone with an imposing stranger. I suddenly wished for Talyssa's presence by my side. She'd been my chaperon countless times.

In an attempt to hide my nervousness, I set my suitcase down and brought my gloved hands together.

"I assure you I mean this as a compliment," Knight Kelsus said, "You are not the type of Challenger we are used to receiving."

I wasn't sure there was anything to say to this, so I pressed my lips together.

"But…" he said, "I'm not here to question your decision. I'm here to weed out the weak from the strong." He said this with a raised eyebrow as if he were trying to tell me he was here to weed *me* out.

"I'm many things," I said, "but weak is not one of them."

To my surprise Knight Kelsus laughed. This was the type of comment that had always earned me disapproving glances from Papa and his friends—male and female alike—but it seemed Knight Kelsus wasn't plagued by their same sensibilities.

"I'm glad to hear that," he said, returning to his seat behind the desk. "Please, sit down, Ms. Flagfall. Let's make this official."

I sat on the chair across from him, placing my hands on my lap and keeping my back ramrod straight, the way my governess had always instructed.

Knight Kelsus smiled again, something he seemed to do a lot, and said, "At least I won't have to teach you to sit straight. You're already a master of that skill, I see."

I smiled a bit, lured by the Knight's easy manner. It felt wrong to do so. Papa was gone, and no mirth should exist when he did not, but I wasn't here to mourn him, was I? I had a role to play and hiding how I truly felt was part of it.

The Knight pulled out a piece of paper and a thin dagger from one of the desk drawers.

"This is the contract that will bind you to the White Queen." He pushed the piece of paper in my direction. "Read it carefully. It must be signed in blood."

My eyes snapped to his. He fingered the dagger and started pushing it in my direction. "You may borrow this."

"No, thank you. I have my own," I said, then pulled Papa's dagger from the hidden spot at my waist.

Knight Kelsus smiled crookedly. "I have a feeling you will do just fine amongst our ranks, Ms. Flagfall."

I looked down at the contract, my thudding heart quieting slightly. Apparently, there would be no test to check my blood, for what Trove would be stupid enough to offer herself as a Challenger.

Taking a deep breath, I read the contract.

After someone became a Challenger, they didn't automatically become Pawns. No. A Challenger had to earn his or her place on the Board. I had known this in the general sense, but the contract made me privy to the exact way the entire process worked.

And it was a more elaborate affair than I had imagined. First, it consisted of competitions between challengers. Before any challenger had a chance to fight to become an actual Pawn, he or she had to beat at least one other challenger. The contests took place under a code of honor where cheating was severely punished. For fairness' sake, Challengers were given eight weeks to prepare.

The contract was long and intimidating to read, but it was the final clause that made me hesitate the most.

"The contract may not be discussed with anyone outside The Board, doing so is punishable by death. Lastly, a Challenger who fails to succeed in becoming a Pawn forfeits their life in benefit of the honorable White Queen if a pardon is not issued by the winner."

In benefit of the honorable White Queen.
In benefit.

The words seemed to jump at me as I read. They were written in black ink just as the rest of them, but in my mind, I saw red. The blood the Queen would take from me for *her benefit.*

"That is the last clause for a reason, Ms. Flagfall," Knight Kelsus said, watching me closely. "Make sure you understand its meaning."

"I believe I do," I said, reminding myself that my life had been forfeited already.

I had no one to go to. The Black King had taken everything from me. No respectable gentleman would marry me without a dowry. And the only person I cared for in the world was in the king's monstrous hands. My life was nothing. I'd thought myself special, important, but I was nobody.

It was only here, inside the enclosure of this White Palace, where I might find a way to change that.

So I pricked my finger with Papa's dagger and, using the quill Knight Kelsus offered, I signed my life away.

6

The next morning, I was given a white uniform like the one Pawns wore, except without an insignia on the right sleeve of the jacket. Wearing trousers was an interesting affair and took some getting used to, but after a short time, I was forced to admit they were much more comfortable than skirts, even if not airy enough for summer.

They didn't make me crop my hair, for which I was glad. I had thought it would be mandatory, but that was not the case. Vinna said that as long as I kept my curls out of my face, no one cared how long they were. So I found a dark piece of leather that matched my brown hair and tied it back at the nape of my neck. As I finished dressing, I found that I missed my makeup and felt a bit naked without it, but I decided that was only a vain discomfort.

"Yeh look sharp," Vinna said as I stepped out from behind the changing screen in our dormitory, a long room with simple cots assigned to the four White Pawns and three Challengers of Knight Kelsus's Quadrant, the second on Queen Lovina's Board.

"So tall and elegant," Vinna said. "I wish I looked half as good." She tugged at her jacket and shuffled in her tall black boots.

"Don't say that, the best perfumes come in the smallest bottles," I told her.

"Huh?" She wrinkled her nose, looking confused.

Did she not know perfume and how expensive the best essences could be? I thought of my favorite fragrances back at home, wishing I could show her what I meant, but pushed the desire away almost as quickly as it reared its head. That life didn't exist anymore, the Bianca who'd loved balls and fancy gowns was dead... or more accurately, was in the process of dying. This new life stabbed me a little bit harder every chance it got.

"So what now?" I asked.

"Breakfast," Vinna said, motioning for me to follow.

We left our Quadrant's dormitory, which was located in a squat building close to the gates and away from the palace itself. A replica of our dormitory was next door, which likely belonged to the Pawns and Challengers in the First Quadrant.

Past that sat two more buildings, quite more spacious than ours. The Rooks' and Knights' dormitories, I imagined.

"Those are the Rook and Knight dormitories," Vinna said, confirming my guess. "The Rooks' are better than ours, actual beds and nicer facilities, but much the same. The Knights is fancy, with a library and rugs and curtains. They have separate rooms. Must be grand, don't yeh think?"

I said nothing. I knew exactly how it could be, but I needed to forget about those types of comforts. They belonged to the rich, and I was poor now, though thankfully I had a roof over my head, clothes, and food. The beauty of the gardens and palace beyond seemed to count, too—at least until I remembered I'd had to stuff bloodshade leaves into my mouth before anyone woke up and discovered what I was. Not to mention the fact that I had signed my life away in blood.

All the dormitories were made of white rock and appeared resplendent under the morning sun. That was until I glanced toward the top of the hill and saw the Queen's Palace sparkling like a giant diamond.

The palace stretched out behind a luscious, labyrinthine garden, and occupied approximately two city squares. It was three stories tall with hundreds of windows on all sides—some of them arched, some of them perfect rectangles. At each end, blue-green copper domes topped four towers that were higher than the rest of the building. Each stone was pristine white, some carved into shapes that gave the structure added interest.

We passed under a large oak with sweeping branches, and I was assaulted by the ridiculous idea of reading a book under its shadow and passing the entire day in fictional bliss.

No more of that, Bianca. Get used to it! I chastised myself.

Instead, I focused on what was important, figuring out how to stay alive by getting to know my competition.

"Did Knight Ferko really decapitate the last Rook who fought for the post of Knight?" I asked. Knight

Ferko ran the First Quadrant and was infamous for his cruelty.

Vinna rolled her eyes. "Folks sure love a villain. Everyone knows Knight Ferko, the Decapitator. But do they know Knight Kelsus? No. Who would remember the man who pardons all poor devils who fight him?" She shook her head.

I swallowed hard. How could I ever hope to defeat a man who chose to decapitate when he could pardon?

"What about the Bishops? Where do they sleep?" I asked.

Vinna pointed toward the palace at the top of the steep hill. "Close to the Queen," she said, lowering her voice. "They're queer folk, those two. Don't like either one of them. If yeh see them, yeh turn tail and run the other way, yeh hear me?"

I nodded. I would worry about the Bishops when the time came. For now, I would have my hands full with learning as much as I could about the four Pawns in Knight Kelsus's Quadrant. It was one of them I had to defeat, which included Vinna. Looking at her sideways, I wondered why she was being so nice. I guessed because before I could get to her I had to beat any Challengers who'd joined the ranks ahead of me.

We made our way to the dining hall, the same building where I'd met Knight Kelsus last night. As soon as Vinna and I entered, everyone went quiet and turned their attention to me. Some regarded me curiously, but most seemed hostile, as if I'd come to steal their breakfast, which, in a way, I had.

At the end of one of the tables, Knight Kelsus rose. "Welcome, Challenger Flagfall."

No more Ms. *Flagfall?* One more reminder that the person I'd once been was dead now.

"Everyone, this is our new Challenger. She signed the contract with me last night, so she is, for the moment, in my Quadrant," Knight Kelsus announced. "Do you wish to contend, Knight Ferko?"

A man at the end of the second table rose to his feet and walked in my direction, his boots clicking against the stone floor, his cropped black hair thick against a pale scalp. He stopped several paces away from me and eyed me up and down. I inhaled deeply and held his red-tinged gaze.

Something about his face made me blink and look closer. The shape was a gentle oval with a narrow chin and a jaw as smooth as a baby's bottom. I startled in surprise. Knight Ferko wasn't a man at all. Knight Ferko was a woman.

She was a few inches taller than me and looked no more than twenty-five, though she had to be much older, kept young by the vampire blood that made her a Knight of the White Court.

"No, I don't want her," Knight Ferko said after assessing me. She waved a dismissive hand in my direction and retook her seat.

Anger stirred in my chest. How could she dismiss me that way after one simple look?

The contract had stated that both White Knights had a right to claim new Challengers. The Knights would first discuss things amicably, and if they didn't reach a decision, the Challenger would then be allowed to choose.

I would have definitely gone with Knight Kelsus over that arrogant, heartless, and… decapitating woman, if asked to choose, but being dismissed so readily certainly hurt my ego.

I turned up my nose and followed Vinna to Knight Kelsus's table.

Sitting with my back toward the wall, I was able to observe Knight Ferko's table and its occupants.

"Bunch of thugs," Vinna said, noticing my interest in the Decapitator's chosen. "You're better off with us." She picked up her plate and began to pile food on it.

I followed her example.

Still intent on the other side, I grabbed a lukewarm roll from a basket and stuck a dab of butter in its center. As I waited for it to melt, I counted four additional females and three males at the opposite table. Three of the females and one male had Pawn insignias on their arms. The others must be Challengers like me, since they bore no insignias.

Forcing myself to forget about the arrogant Decapitator, I focused on breakfast and observing my group. There were two male Pawns and two female, including Vinna, plus two male Challengers.

I eyed them surreptitiously. I had to defeat one of them, but which? How would I do it? What test would be set out for us? They were chosen at random, according to the contract.

One of the Challengers caught my eye. He was close to my age, thick as a fattened pig and with little beady eyes and bristled brown hair to match. He bared his teeth and slid a finger across his throat.

I glanced away, a sudden stab of fear piercing my heart.

Oh, dear!

What had I gotten myself into? I wasn't good at anything besides dancing and fanning myself, and I doubted either one of those talents counted for anything. Would eight weeks be enough to get me ready for the challenge?

I clenched my fists, making the small wound on my finger smart. I had signed the contract with my blood. That had to count for something. I was brave. My heart beat strong and willfully in my chest. It always had. I would make that count, too.

I had eight weeks before I needed to prove myself, and I intended to do everything within my power to learn what I could during that time.

7

Knight Kelsus might have been all smiles and manners at meal time, but he was a despot the rest of the time. He had the audacity to make us run. Run! Of all things, and in senseless circles, no less.

His Pawns—Breen, Petru, Vinna, and Alben—were practically gazelles, galloping up and down the hills behind the palace, a forest as thick as the hairs on my head. In fact, they were all gazelles, even the other Challengers—Miron and Skender, the pig-looking one—while I was nothing but a decrepit turtle without hopes of ever making it to the finish line.

I pressed a hand against a tree and leaned forward, my breakfast of hard cheese and bacon threatening to reappear.

Today, I'd been a little better than a week ago, but I was still last. My shirt was soaked in sweat, something I would never get used to, and my feet throbbed inside my leather boots. The only good thing was that the blisters on my small toes were healing since I'd finally broken in the boots as Vinna said I would, which suddenly reminded me I had somewhere to be.

I ran away from the trees and into the open. Alben had said I would start sword practice with him and Vinna today, though I didn't know how I would survive more exercise. Making people get so breathless should be against the law. I was sure my heart only had so many beats to give, and this week's training had stolen half of them.

Heart thudding some more, I got to the sparring field to the west of the White Palace. I was still only seeing the building from a distance, but in the daylight, its ivory magnificence was dazzling.

The best feature, in my opinion, was the large fountain out front. It was surrounded by white statues of forest nymphs and a labyrinth of perfectly kept hedges and flower beds around it.

"Yeh're late," Alben pointed out as I came to a halt in front of him and doubled over, panting. "If yeh're late tomorrow, yeh will have to go back and run again."

"What? That's not fair," I protested.

Alben raised his thick eyebrows, looking unamused. His demeanor wasn't friendly at all—not like it had been up to this point. I straightened to attention, another thing I'd quickly learned after Knight Kelsus had made me muck out horse poop in the stables when he caught me smiling at a butterfly instead of listening to him ramble about the proper way to care for my horse, an ugly brown beast he'd assigned to me.

Maybe Alben had finally decided I was a real Challenger, and I could soon take his spot, while he was be sent back home. In the last week, I had learned he was the newest Pawn in Knight Kelsus's Quadrant, therefore the one I'd have to challenge if I became the top Challenger, a post currently occupied by Miron.

Vinna came over and handed each of us a sword. It was long and thin with a protective hilt for my hand. Good, at least I wouldn't lose my fingers.

Alben gripped his sword and held it straight up, the blade creating two symmetrical halves of his bearded face. He inclined his head, staring pointedly at my sword.

Understanding his meaning, I mimicked him. He watched my posture and nodded approvingly. Next, he kicked a foot back, bent his knees, and extended the sword, aiming it straight at my heart.

He gestured for me to do the same. I complied.

My heart beat faster. Would Alben cut me? The contract specified that no one could kill me during training, but it didn't rule out cutting or even maiming.

But I was wrong to be scared because our blades never touched. Instead, Alben simply guided me through a series of poses that he silently encouraged me to imitate. Not a word passed between us, and to my amazement, I found the exercise calming and graceful.

"It seems yeh're a natural at this," Alben said in his usual cheerful tone as we finished our lesson.

"It *was* easy," I said, surprised. "Almost like dancing, which I'm definitely good at—but that was far from a real sword fight."

Alben shrugged. "Form's important. The rest should come to yeh."

"Alben's right," Vinna said as we headed away from the palace and back toward our dormitory.

I smiled, feeling a bit more hopeful, so far I'd been terrible at running and even worse at riding that beast they called a horse. The four-legged creature had to be a mule in disguise, considering how stubborn it was. It was nice to be good at something.

"Not that I'm complaining," I said, "but why are you two being so nice to me?"

"Teaching yeh is our duty, Bianca," Vinna said. "Part of our Pawn contracts."

Pawn contracts? There must be a contract at every level, I realized. I stored the information in my growing bank of facts.

"I doubt this contract states you should do it nicely," I said. "I've seen how some of the other Pawns treat the other Challengers. They shoot daggers at me with their eyes every time I pass by."

"They're insecure," Alben said, peering firmly in my direction. "We know we could take yeh in a challenge."

I felt the blood drain from my face. Even though I'd tried to, I couldn't imagine facing Alben. His arms were as thick as tree trunks, and he was so tall. He could break me like a twig. Besides, I liked him.

Vinna and Alben exchanged a glance, then burst out laughing.

"I's just kidding, little lady," Alben said, patting his middle as he laughed. "Vinna and me just follow a different philosophy, that's all."

"We're here for good," Vinna added. "Some Challenger or another will show up at the gate every so often, and we'll have to go through all of this with them. I've seen a handful come through, and I've only been here two years. Now, we could be mad at them all the time, and we could walk around as if we have a sword up our rears…"

I gasped at her rude comment, then held back a giggle.

"Or…" she continued, "while it lasts, we could enjoy being Pawns and having steady Chekes to send our families, and living here." She extended her arms out and turned in a circle. "Tell me what's the better option?"

"You have a point," I said.

My own disposition had always been a positive one, so I could understand Vinna's reasoning. But lately, there had been nothing but gloom in my thoughts, and even though Vinna tried to cheer me up, my mind was quick to wander to a dark place where Papa's blank stare haunted me, and Talyssa's voice cried out in anguish, begging for rescue and respite from the monster who had taken her.

Alben and Vinna were happy as Pawns. They'd come here with nothing else in mind but becoming members of the White Queen's exclusive Board, and they'd gotten what they wanted. I, on the other hand, had come here for an entirely different reason, and becoming a Pawn was only the beginning.

"Costin and Sorinna will face each other today," Vinna announced, breaking me out of my thoughts.

I snapped back to attention. This would be my first opportunity to witness a challenge and see what awaited me.

Costin and Sorinna were in Knight Ferko's Quadrant. The former was the top Challenger. He had been here the longest, waiting for Sorinna to complete her eight weeks of training. If he defeated her, he would then be allowed to challenge the Fourth Pawn in the Decapitator's Quadrant. If he lost, then Sorinna would take his place to become the top Challenger.

It was an elaborate process that ensured only the best joined the Queen's Board. The contract had spelled it all out and Vinna had clarified it for me. She said that, for the most part, once you became a Pawn, your chances of staying there were good. Most of the time, Challengers simply knocked each other out, and few ever managed to challenge a Pawn. If they did make it that far, they found that defeating a Pawn was much harder than defeating a Challenger, since Pawns had been training much longer and the majority were seasoned veterans.

"Do you think Sorinna can beat him?" I asked.

Vinna shrugged. "It will depend on the type of challenge."

The contract had mentioned the challenges were chosen at random, but there hadn't been any specifics as to the type of fight, so I had no idea what to expect, and no one had been forthcoming about the details, not even Vinna.

"Well, Sorinna seems quick on her feet," I said, fishing for information, but Vinna just gave me a crooked smile.

"Half the fun is in not knowing, little lady," Alben said, tapping the side of his nose.

8

"What are they doing now?" I leaned to my left to whisper in Vinna's ear.

"Be quiet and watch," she scolded.

It was the second time she'd declined to answer me, but being quiet and observing hadn't led me anywhere, not for the past ten minutes we'd been sitting here.

We were in a large square room with a tall ceiling and elongated windows high up on the walls. We were sitting on chairs atop a dais, while across from us, Knight Ferko's Pawns and Challengers occupied a similar space, ready to observe the challenge from prime positions. Opposite the entrance, a third dais with a small throne dominated the entire room—a place for Queen Lovina, I presumed. In the center of the floor, the checked pattern of a chessboard had been carefully painted. The place was known as the Challenge Hall.

The Knights were nowhere in sight. I'd thought they would be here to make sure everything went as it was supposed to, but apparently, when they had other obligations, that was a job for their Pawns.

Trying my best to do as Vinna had instructed, I watched Costin and Sorinna walk to a tall stone pedestal that stood midway between both daises. A white vase sat atop the pedestal, and without preamble, Costin reached a hand inside it and pulled something out. He held it out to Sorinna.

I craned my neck to see it was a small box. Sorinna held it on her open palm and stared at it a moment too long. Costin—a slender man no more than twenty-five—smiled with satisfaction, probably taking Sorinna's pause as a sign of fear. Though judging by her calm face and careful demeanor, her pause made me think she felt confident.

Just when Costin was starting to appear aggravated, Sorinna opened the small box and pulled out a white chess piece.

Holding it up between her thumb and forefinger, Sorinna said, "A Rook."

Costin and Sorinna turned and bowed toward their Quadrant, then retreated to a corner to remove their jackets.

A Rook? What did that mean? I scratched my head, confused. I wanted to ask Vinna, but she would probably shush me again.

"The Rook means they have to wrestle," Skender said from my left. His beady eyes seemed full of malice. "That stupid girl doesn't stand a chance. Maybe if they'd gotten a Knight or even a Pawn, but a Rook…" He laughed.

"I politely disagree," I said. "And she's not a *girl*. Sorinna's a woman."

"Same thing," he said with a sneer. "What do you care anyway? They're on the Decapitator's Quadrant, not ours."

I shrugged one shoulder and sent a disdainful glance his way. "Female pride," I said, then turned away, signaling that our conversation was over.

The Rook means they have to wrestle, Skender had said.

I'd had no other choice but to stand for Sorinna. I made it a point to always defend other women. We already had enough men always trying to put us down and *keep* us down. So I felt it was my duty to stand for my sex whenever necessary. But wrestling? How barbaric! Couldn't they have a challenge to see who could finish their embroidery first? Why did men always have to have the advantage? Costin was taller and stronger than Sorinna. As much as I'd like to think she did, Sorinna didn't stand a chance.

After removing their jackets, the Challengers proceeded to remove their boots as well. My heart raced in fear for Sorinna. Even if she was in the Decapitator's Quadrant, she seemed nice. I was sure that if Costin defeated her, he wouldn't choose to pardon her. He didn't seem like the type.

Moving back toward the center, the challengers faced each other, crouching low in attack positions. Everyone watched quietly, no words of encouragement offered to either one of them.

My heart skipped a beat as Costin lunged forward, attempting to wrap his arms around Sorinna's legs. Quick as lightning, she dodged out of the way and sent a sideways kick into her opponent's side.

I almost clapped excitedly as Costin fell to the floor, but he recovered quickly, rolling away from Sorinna and jumping back to his feet. He growled angrily, his teeth bared like an animal's. For her part, Sorinna smiled, which only seemed to enrage Costin further.

For several minutes, the fight went on in the same fashion: Costin attacking and Sorinna finding a way to evade him. I hated to admit it, but watching them brawl had me in an excited state, more intense than any I'd experienced at any of the balls I'd ever attended, even the Hallows Eve masquerade last year.

Every time she got away, I wanted to cheer for Sorinna, but since it didn't seem appropriate, I focused on her technique and concluded that strength wasn't everything. Costin's muscles were proving useless against Sorinna's speed and cleverness. Moreover, her patient approach was driving Costin mad, so much that his rage had started causing him to make idiotic mistakes.

"I'm going to kill yeh, whore," Costin screamed, running at Sorinna like a mad bull. His face was red, and his voice rumbled with ire.

Calmly, Sorinna waited till the last possible instant, then using Costin's own momentum against him, grabbed one of his arms, hefted him over her back, and flipped him to the stone floor.

Costin fell with a bone-cracking *thud*. He groaned and stayed down for a moment, then got up slowly, pulling a knife from some hidden place on his person.

I gasped as the knife's blade glinted, reflecting the light from one of the high windows. Sorinna took a step back, her eyes wide and questioning.

Was a knife allowed?

My answer came immediately as all eight Pawns vacated their seats, descended the daises, and stood between the Challengers.

"You have broken the rules," Yessenia, one of Knight Ferko's Pawns, said. "Your contract is forfeit."

Pulling out the sword at her waist and twirling it with skill and precision, she quickly disarmed Costin. His knife went flying up in the air, then clattered to the floor with finality.

"Let's take him away," Yessenia said. "Knight Ferko will deal with him."

Without another word, the Decapitator's Quadrant left, taking Costin with him. Sorinna followed them after picking up the rook piece Costin had taken out of the vase. She clenched it tightly in her hand and walked out with her head held high.

9

A couple of weeks passed in a flurry of running around the same stretch of forest, sword sparring with Alben and Vinna, and mucking out my stubborn horse's stall after trying unsuccessfully to ride it—not to mention the required reading that bored me to death, since I was already familiar with all the books: tales of how Acedrex came to be, as well as biographies of all the city's previous monarchs.

As far as the horse went, Vinna insisted it was my fault the animal didn't do what it was supposed to, but how was that possible? I was a rational being, while the beast was just that, a beast.

I disliked the creature. Horrible, hard spots had formed in the palms of my hands because I was forced to clean its waste. It was... humiliating.

And how did the beast repay me? It disobeyed me at every turn. The ungrateful good-for-nothing!

Like right now, while everyone circled around the track—a large oval path with a patch of beautiful grass in the middle—the brown monstrosity was walking up to the fence to eat weeds, like usual.

I growled in frustration.

"The other way," I said, pulling on its reins, but I might as well been pulling on a house.

Urging the beast, I did everything short of beating it to make it move. As much as I disliked the animal, I couldn't bring myself to use the crop on its fat rump—not when I saw the relish with which the likes of Skender beat his own beast. I refused to turn into a monster. Sure, if I succeeded in my plan I was guaranteed to become one, but I didn't intend to hurry the process along.

"Move, horse," I said, bouncing on the saddle and kicking my heels.

Nothing.

The others galloped several laps by the time I managed a single one.

It was the same every day: wake up at five in the morning, eat the same food, follow the same training routine.

Running had gone from entirely too difficult to bearable. I even promoted myself to baby gazelle since I was able to finish the route in a decent time, even if I was still last.

Training with the sword was definitely my favorite since, as Alben had predicted, I was an absolute natural. All I had to do every time we sparred was imagine myself dancing the minuet, going from one partner to another, waving my hand with grace and accuracy, and it all went perfectly. I'd even managed to touch Alben with the blunt tip of my sword a few times, and just yesterday, I had caught him and Vinna exchanging a concerned glance. Could it be that they were starting to see me as a worthy Challenger, after all? I certainly hoped so.

If only I could master this obstinate horse, or if Knight Kelsus would agree to let me have a different one. But he'd said my chestnut mare was a fine animal. Was he even paying attention? The thing didn't even prance, much less gallop. Obviously, he didn't care.

Later that day, exhausted after the morning exercises, I sighed and bit into a piece of overcooked ham. It was lunch time, and we sat in the dining hall, enjoying the break from duties more than the food. I missed Louisa's cooking as well as her comforting presence. Talyssa and I had loved sitting in the kitchen, watching her knead the dough for her delicious yeast rolls. It was relaxing and provided us with the perfect opportunity to press her for the gossip she heard from servants of neighboring families—especially gossip that involved eligible gentlemen.

I sighed again and pushed my plate away.

"What's wrong, Bianca?" Vinna asked, shoving a piece of pink ham into her already full mouth.

"Oh, nothing, just tired." It wasn't the whole truth, but then I was always exhausted these days.

"Then yeh'll love to hear we've the rest of the day off."

I perked up at this. "We do?"

She mumbled a *yes*, then after swallowing, she added, "We get paid too, which is no coincidence. They want us to spend our few Chekes as soon as we get them."

"Don't be so jaded, Vinna," Alben said as he screwed his eyes, trying to look at his beard. He had a piece of food tangled in it.

I shook my head. He was always doing that. Honestly, he needed to get rid of the thing, but he wouldn't have it. He said his beard was his pride and joy. It gave him "personality." I politely disagreed. Nothing that could serve as a home *and* dinner to mice should be anyone's pride and joy.

"Not true," Vinna said. "I've four mouths to feed. You only worry 'bout yehr hefty self." She poked him in the belly.

"Hefty? This is all muscle, I'll have you know." Alben straightened and sucked in his stomach, patting it with as much pride as he displayed when stroking his beard.

Turning my attention to Vinna, I asked, "So we actually get to go out?" The contract had mentioned something about time off, but again, there had been no details.

"That, we do."

"Oh, thank goodness. I desperately need a distraction," I said, while thinking of the real reason I wanted to go into Acedrex: bloodshade.

I still had enough to last me a few more weeks, but finding a steady supply of the bitter leaves was crucial to my survival in this place.

As some of my long-lost enthusiasm returned, so did my appetite. I pulled the plate back and finished my meal, looking forward to the freedom I'd relinquished the moment I stepped into the White Palace.

10

All Pawns and Challengers filed through the White Palace's gates in a hurry.

Petru, the Second Pawn in my Quadrant, stretched his hands to the heavens and let out a relieved *ahhh*. He was a tall and slender young man of about twenty, with black, curly hair and gray eyes. I didn't know much about him, but he appeared to have been raised in a fairly prosperous environment, judging by the lilt and pattern of his speech.

"I've been waiting for this day like a vampire waits for Trove's blood," he said.

I stiffened and did my best to appear unaffected by the comment. I'd heard the saying plenty of times before, but now it carried an entirely different connotation for me.

Beside Petru, Breen and Skender stood next to each other, matching sly smiles stretching their lips. They glanced at each other sideways, their hands hanging at their sides, barely a millimeter away from touching. I raised an eyebrow. I had seen similar displays between clandestine couples at many of the balls I'd attended since my coming out. A relationship between members of the Board was forbidden. They would be in deep trouble if anyone found out.

Before I could look away and quell my surprise, Breen turned in my direction and caught me spying. I smiled, trying to act as if I hadn't noticed anything out of the ordinary, but she didn't fall for it. Her eyes narrowed, mouth twisting in a crooked sneer. She seemed furious.

I turned to Vinna and made some inconsequential comment about the weather as we started our descent from the palace toward the sprawling, checkered section of Acedrex.

Below, the streets ran north to south, perfectly parallel to each other. The avenues cut across, forming a grid, which made dividing the city into black and white squares much easier.

Just to help the Black King and White Queen keep better watch of their respective dominions, buildings located on black squares had black roofs, while the rest had white ones.

The city's order was pleasing and chilling at them same time, especially when the expansive wall that surrounded Acedrex was taken into account. It was as tall as five men, built on the backs and sweat of human slaves hundreds and hundreds of years ago. No one went beyond it without explicit permission from the King or Queen, and no one came past its gates to stay unless the population dwindled. Of course, merchants were allowed in. They brought their desirable goods and got valuable Chekes in return. Then, they went back to wherever they came from, looking sad to leave and eager to come back.

Beyond the wall, there were mountains, rocky, ominous and daunting. I could only imagine what lay beyond them.

Across from the White Palace, on a hill on the other side of the city, sat King Maximus's lair. The structure was ominous, black as his heart, and the manors that flanked it seemed to cower under its menacing shadows.

We were halfway to the city when Breen approached me and surreptitiously pulled me away from Vinna and Alben.

When we were out of earshot, she said in a venomous tone, "I don't like yeh, *Challenger*."

A biting answer jumped to the tip of my tongue, but I held it back. Being on the First Pawn's bad side was not good for any Challenger, especially a Trove like me. I didn't want Breen casting too much of her toxic attention in my direction.

So, I swallowed my bitter retort and, instead, said, "I'm sorry to hear that. I will do my best not to do *anything* that might... bother you."

Her right eye twitched. "That's right smart of yeh, 'cause I can make yehr life hell, if I want to."

"I'm sure you could," I said, my pride tied up in a burning ball in the center of my chest. It was very hard not to give her a piece of my mind.

Skender joined us, leaving me walking between the two of them.

Vinna glanced back, her green eyes searching for me. When she spotted me, she frowned and nudged

Alben, who also seemed displeased with my situation. They casually slowed their pace.

"You don't stand a chance against me. I can't wait to crush you," Skender said.

My heart sped up, drumming against my ribs, a clear sign that I didn't disagree with the brutish Challenger. He was built like a boulder, squat and compact. He could crush me like a street rat under the wheel of a carriage. I inhaled deeply, trying to quiet my traitorous heart. I hadn't come here to lose. I'd come here because of a bully like him.

Still, I measured my words. "And, perhaps, you will crush me."

"Or maybe I'll pardon you, if you're a good girl," he said with a glint in his little eyes.

So he was offering me a bribe to keep my mouth shut about what I'd seen. Too bad I seemed to have a death wish.

"Breen! Skender!" Alben said in an enthusiastic tone, turning to face us. "Want to join us for a tall tankard of ale, mates?"

Breen huffed and gave Alben and Vinna a condescending once-over. With that as her only answer, she walked away from us, Skender quick at her heels.

"What was that about?" Vinna asked, looking at the bullies from beneath a furrowed brow.

"It was nothing," I said, putting on a smile. "Just typical Skender, trying to intimidate me about the challenge."

It was part of the truth, and they seemed to buy it.

After that, we made our way down the rest of the hill in silence, while I tried to focus on the only thing that mattered today: acquiring more bloodshade.

11

We were required to wear our uniforms during our outing to the city, white cloak, sword, and all. At first, I found it strange and missed my wide dress and fan as I moved about the cobbled streets. In the past, I had enjoyed the furtive glances and happy smiles of passing gentlemen as Talyssa and I walked arm-in-arm, while shopping or calling on friends.

Not surprisingly, the court uniform produced an entirely different reaction. No one looked at us, and people even crossed the street to avoid us.

"How rude," I said, as a middle-aged couple turned back the way they'd come when they saw Vinna, Alben, and me approaching.

Vinna shrugged. "Yeh get used to it."

"It's not like we've tasted Queen Lovina's blood," I said.

Everybody knew Pawns and Challengers remained entirely human. Though maybe they suspected *something* went on: a demonic ceremony, perhaps. Gods knew I'd imagined similar things before I joined. But surprisingly, my life inside the palace grounds had been nothing like I'd imagined.

We crossed the street. On the next corner, a white post indicated we were about to enter one of the city squares controlled by Queen Lovina. As we stepped out of the black square we'd been traversing, I breathed a sigh of relief. It was stupid. Unless there was trouble, there was little difference between being on white square or a black one. Still, I couldn't help but loathe anything that belonged to the Black King.

We passed a Sentry post where men and women in white uniforms saluted us by extending their hands toward the ground. It felt strange since I was not even a member of the White Board. They were surely better trained than me and would have better chances at becoming Pawns, but few were as foolish and desperate as I was. Signing your life away to a vampire was as good as making an appointment with death.

Shops—a tailor, a toy store, a furrier, a shoemaker, a milliner, and others—lined the street. The sight of them sent a pang of nostalgia through me. I'd visited most of these establishments in the past, accompanied by Papa or Talyssa. I sighed and pushed the feeling away.

My initial displeasure at wearing the uniform quickly turned to relief when I caught sight of Regina Preendale, my archenemy. She was Archibald Preendale's daughter, a vapid, empty-headed seventeen-year-old girl who gave the rest of the female population a bad name with her actions.

She attended every ball in Acedrex, and invariably managed to get the attention of most eligible men present. Mistakenly, she always assumed it was because of her charms, though the size of her dowry was the real prize.

Regina and her lady-help—her arms loaded with several hat boxes—had just exited Jane Golding's Millinery and turned in our direction. I started and began to hide my face, but at that point, doing so would only have called attention to myself. So instead, I straightened and kept walking.

To my relief, Regina didn't recognize me. Her perpetually wide green eyes rolled off me as if I were nothing but an old piece of furniture, and she went past without a second glance.

I breathed a sigh of relief. The gods only knew what rumors or truths were flying around in our social circles about what had happened at Flagfall House. Did they think I was dead, too? If they did, I surely wanted it to remain that way for now.

"I'm sure she *needed* every one of those hats," Vinna said bitterly.

Embarrassed, I thought of all the hats I had possessed, and all the others I had wished to be able to purchase. Now, the sight of the millinery's colorful window displays only filled me with sadness. It had only been three weeks, but that life seemed to be a million years away now. I had calluses on my hands from holding the sword and mucking out horse excrement, and my brown hair was turning lighter as the sun bleached its rich color. I had even started to enjoy the comfort of my boots as opposed to the toe-pinching agony of women's shoes. Who would have thought?

"First stop, The Bad Bishop," Alben announced, immediately crossing the street toward that popular tavern.

I had never been in such a place, even though I'd always wanted to see inside. Ladies didn't frequent those types of establishments, but Challengers and Pawns... that was another matter.

I checked with Vinna, who simply shrugged, as was her habit, and followed after Alben. "I could use a tankard myself."

We entered the tavern, and I was surprised to find it so full at this hour. It was barely five in the afternoon, and almost every table was occupied.

"Great, Blackies," Vinna said, her mouth twisting in displeasure. Still, she pressed forward, following Alben toward the only empty table.

I stiffened at the sight of all the black uniforms. It seemed King Maximus's Pawns also had the day off. I stuck close to Vinna, telling myself there was no reason to be nervous. These Pawns didn't know me, and even if they did, they probably wouldn't recognize me. Regina hadn't, and she was a hawk, able to spot her targets from across a crowded ballroom without fail.

Once seated, a boy of about thirteen took our orders and quickly returned with three frothing tankards. I stared at my drink distrustfully. I had never drunk more than a few sips of wine and had found its intoxicating properties disconcerting. Talyssa, on the other, loved wine and always complained I had control issues, which didn't allow me to fully enjoy myself.

"There's that look again," Vinna said, pointing at me.

"Missing someone, little lady," Alben asked.

"I guess," I said, picking up my tankard and taking a sip. The ale was chilled and went down my throat smoothly, more easily than any wine ever had.

As I set the tankard down, I noticed that the intense gaze of one the Blackies was set on me. It took me a moment to recognize him, dressed, as he was, in the straight-lined uniform, but I finally recalled where I'd seen him before.

It was the tart thief.

Nyro.

I blinked, surprised that I still remembered his name.

We stared into each other's eyes for a long time, while my mind twirled with questions. The thief was a Blackie? A Challenger like me, judging by the lack of insignia on his sleeve? No, that didn't make sense. If he lived on King Maximus's Palace grounds, he wouldn't need to steal. We always had plenty of food, and I was sure it was the same at the Black Palace. So he must have joined recently, like me. Had he gotten tired of being a thief? Of going hungry?

His dark eyes were stern and unrelenting. I wanted to look away, but damn me if I was going to let him win. Stealing was wrong, and he could be mad at me all he wanted for calling the Sentries on him. I had done the right thing. As I stared, I couldn't help but notice how different he looked in his uniform and tidy trimmed hair and beard. Gods, he was devilishly handsome!

"What now, Bianca?" Vinna asked, following my gaze. After spotting the object of my interest, she turned back, frowning. "You know that Blackie?"

"No," I said, finally looking away and telling myself he hadn't won. I'd just gotten tired of the stupid game.

"Costin's dead," Alben whispered, leaning closer, his eyes darting from side to side to make sure no one heard him.

"Poor devil," Vinna said. "Can't say I'm surprised, though. That was a stupid thing he did. Sorinna would've let him live, I'm sure. How did you find out, anyway?"

Alben tapped his nose. "Can't reveal my sources, but Knight Ferko presented him to Queen Lovina. She made dinner outta him."

A chill ran up my spine. If I didn't become a Pawn, I could end up like Costin. It was one of the darkest clauses in the contract, one of the many I tended to ignore, pretending it didn't exist. If you weren't pardoned, you could end up as the Queen's dinner, much worse than the alternative of dying at your opponent's hand. But no matter.

I would soon become a Pawn, and a plan for my success was already taking shape in my mind.

First things first, though, if I intended to remain in the palace grounds for any length of time, I had to find a reliable supply of bloodshade.

12

For the better part of an hour, I encouraged Vinna and Alben to drink their ale, while I took small sips of mine.

Vinna talked about her family, and how much she missed her sisters, her anecdotes about them getting more colorful the more she drank.

Alben seemed happy to simply listen as he enjoyed his tankard, barely paying attention to anything else.

When their faces had acquired an air of contentment and leisure, I stood and told them I needed to stretch my legs for a while. They weren't instructed to keep me under supervision. I was allowed to go on my own if I wanted, but I didn't want them to get suspicious about my errand.

I liked Vinna and Alben, but I couldn't trust anyone with a secret like mine. The Queen and King paid large rewards to those who brought them Troves, and there was nothing more tempting to humans than the promise of riches.

I left the tavern fully aware of Nyro's eyes on me as I walked out. Once outside, I strolled down the street, casting glances over my shoulder to make sure my friends had stayed behind.

After two blocks, I relaxed and turned in the direction of the White Market. I passed in front of Castling Park, where a few couples strolled easily down the path, one of them walking a squat bulldog on a leash. I smiled sadly at the sight, feeling so far removed from the type of life I once dreamed of.

The trees above rustled with a gentle breeze, and I closed my eyes, suddenly aware that I was alone under the darkening sky. I had never gone anywhere without Papa or Talyssa, much less in the evening. Maybe I should have been worried, but the sword at my waist, and the fact that I knew how to wield it, if only marginally, gave me comfort. Instead, I felt exhilarated. Being out and about when respectable ladies were supposed to be locked behind heavy doors was a type of freedom I'd never enjoyed. Was this how men felt all the time? Safe wherever they went?

Leaving my nostalgic reverie behind, I pressed forward. When I turned the corner on the street where the market usually set up every day, I found—to my utter disappointment and panic—that most vendors had already left. The few that remained sold no more than nonperishable goods such as pots and brooms, and even they were gathering their wares. The ones that sold herbs and teas were long gone. All the stores around the market also appeared closed, their window displays dark.

I cursed under my breath, a word Papa would have been scandalized to hear on my lips, but one that I heard often inside the palace grounds.

Pausing for a moment, I wondered what to do. I should have guessed the market would be closed this late. Instead, I had wasted all afternoon with Vinna and Alben.

As I stood there cursing my stupidity, I noticed movement inside one of the brick and mortar stores: the apothecary's shop. My heart leapt with relief as I hurried across the street.

A bell rang above the door as I opened it. Mr. Oakes—a heavy-set man of about fifty, dressed in a black vest and shirtsleeves—stood behind a wooden counter, where he was transferring a white substance from a large container into smaller ones. He was intent on his work, just like all the other times I'd been here with Talyssa to purchase Papa's headache powders.

"Good evening," I said.

"Oh," he said in surprise, watching me from above round spectacles. "I must have forgotten to affix the 'closed' sign."

"Please, it won't take but a moment. Um… I just…"

Now that I was here, doubt crept into my chest like a giant spider. Was this safe? What if telling this man what I needed landed me right on King Maximus's lap, stealing my chance for revenge?

And yet… what other choice did I have?

"Um…" I took a step closer, lowering my voice. "I'm looking for bloodshade leaves."

The apothecary set down the container he was holding and looked me up and down, his expression guarded.

"I'm… sorry, but I don't carry *that*, ma'am," he said, his tone sounding a lot like Papa's when he lied.

I paused, my eyes darting over the dozens of bottles that sat on the shelves behind him, desperately trying to read each label, which was stupid because he wouldn't have such a thing out in the open, just like he wouldn't sell it to someone wearing a white uniform.

Where had Papa purchased my bloodshade? I wished he had told me.

Perhaps I was taking a great risk confiding in this man, but if I didn't get any bloodshade today, my stint as a Challenger would come to an abrupt end anyway.

Tentatively, I walked closer to the counter.

"Mr. Oakes," I said. "I'm Bianca Flagfall. Remember me? Papa, Martin Flagfall, used to purchase his medicine from you."

His eyes widened, and he examined my face with more care. Finally, he spoke, his face going pale. "You poor girl. Everyone thinks you… that King Maximus…" he was unable to finish.

I clenched my teeth in a effort to keep back the tears that threatened to spill.

"But," he regarded my uniform with undisguised distaste, "you're with the White Queen."

"I had no other choice," I said. "King Maximus took everything from me. Papa, Talyssa who was like a sister to me, my fortune, everything. I did what I had to do." I lifted my chin high.

Mr. Oakes nodded in understanding. His gray eyes were gentle, and something about the way he looked at me made me think he had daughters of his own, daughters he would protect with his life if it came to it.

"Would you help me, please?" I begged.

"I… really wish I could, Ms. Flagfall, but I'm afraid I don't have what you're looking for."

I still thought he was lying, protecting himself, but how could I blame him? We all knew what the vampire monarchy was capable of. I had seen it firsthand. If he was discovered selling bloodshade, he would suffer Papa's fate or possibly worse. The tears that had pooled in my eyes spilled onto my cheeks as I lowered my head.

"I understand," I said, turning to leave.

At the door, I dried my eyes, took a deep breath, and turned the knob.

"Wait!" Mr. Oakes said.

My heart froze. I slowly turned to face him, hope building in my chest. He examined my face carefully, as if considering one last time whether or not he could trust me.

"Don't go anywhere," he said as he turned and disappeared through a door in the back of his store.

I fidgeted on the spot until he returned a few minutes later. I searched his hands, but they were empty. I frowned. He gestured for me to move toward the corner furthest from the window.

I stood in front of him, the wide wooden counter between us. Quickly, he produced a pouch from his breast pocket and passed it across the counter.

"Put it away. Quickly."

I did as instructed, stuffing the pouch through the buttons of my jacket.

My chest swelled with gratitude. "Thank you," I said in a whisper.

"Don't let anyone see you with it," he adamantly instructed.

"I won't."

"It is foolish for you to remain with the White Queen. You should hide. Get as far away as possible from those monsters."

That idea was a constant visitor in my mind, especially at night when I lay awake on my cot, recalling my evening conversations with Papa and Talyssa, the easy way we'd laughed together, and the peace we'd shared. But when I realized it had all been a lie, that the world we lived in was cruel, and the horrors I thought only happened to others were just a carriage ride away, I understood I couldn't hide. Being at the palace gave me a worthy purpose. I had a goal. I would one day have my revenge. Fleeing would only leave me aimless.

"I can't," I said. "The contract binds me, now. They would kill me if I break it."

This was something Mr. Oakes would understand: fear. My foolish idea of revenge, he would laugh at.

I took a few coins from my pocket and displayed them in my palm. "How much do I owe you?"

He shook his head. "It's nothing. Bloodshade is a weed that grows easily. But…" He turned to the shelf to his right, retrieved a small, square packet from a box, and handed it to me. "This is smartweed. All the girls in the White Board and Black Board purchase it. If anyone asks why you were here, you can tell them you came in for this."

"What does it do?" I asked.

Mr. Oakes flushed. "It prevents you from getting with child."

"Oh!"

My cheeks grew so hot I felt like a street lamp. "I… I won't need this." I tried to give it back.

"Keep it," he said firmly. "It's the perfect excuse."

"I see." I put the small paper packet away.

"Ten Chekes," he said, all business now.

I paid him and thanked him again.

"When you need more," he said, returning to the work I'd interrupted when I first came, "come at the same time and wait until no one is inside."

I nodded and thanked him one more time, but he wasn't paying attention anymore. He had dismissed me and seemed ready to be rid of me. He had more than one reason to want me out of his store. One, I was wearing the White Queen's uniform. Two, I was a Trove.

We had a right to distrust each other. Though perhaps I was the one taking the bigger risk. One word from him, and I would end up a slave. But I had no other choice but to trust him. Without bloodshade, I would be discovered anyway. But what about him? The few Chekes he'd taken from me wouldn't make him rich. So why would he risk so much for someone he barely knew?

With a bow, I turned and left Oakes Apothecary. The bell above the door tinkled as I left, a gentle sound that punctuated my desperate desire to run and hide the proof of my crime.

13

I crossed the street away from the apothecary at a fast clip, so intent on getting back to The Bad Bishop that I didn't notice the dark figure hiding under the shade of one of the opposing buildings.

Guided by instincts I didn't know I had acquired, my hand flew to the sword at my waist. I was about to draw it out when I recognized the would-be assailant.

Nyro.

"Hello," he said as if we were acquaintances, but I didn't befriend thieves... or Blackies.

I narrowed my eyes at him, trying to ignore how he cut an impressive figure in his black uniform. Instead, I twisted my mouth in distaste, a message to let him know I wanted nothing to do with him. Then, hand still on the hilt of my sword, I continued on my way.

"You joined the Whities and lost your manners?" he asked, matching my step down the sidewalk.

"Thieves demanding manners," I mused. "What nerve!"

"I have to say, the uniform suits you." He leaned back, taking a suggestive look at my posterior.

Outraged, I whirled and slapped him, or at least I tried. He was too fast and caught my wrist before my hand could connect with his face. I pulled away, anger swelling in my chest. He was smiling crookedly, regarding me with amusement.

"Leave me alone," I growled and continued on.

He walked by my side as I tried to ignore him. If I didn't talk to him, he would get bored and leave me alone.

My patience only lasted to Castling Park.

"Stop following me!" I demanded.

"I'm not following you," he said. "I'm walking right next to you. Besides, you should be grateful. A lady shouldn't be out by herself at this hour."

"Thief. Challenger. Protector," I said in a mocking tone. "You certainly are multifaceted."

"I do my best," he said.

I rolled my eyes and gestured toward my sword. "I do not need your *protection*."

"You do… if you are purchasing bloodshade."

My mouth went dry. "I… I don't know what you're talking about."

He smiled knowingly and resumed walking, leaving me standing there, blinking at a park bench.

How did he know? Who would he tell? He was nothing but a thief. He would become a rich man if he turned me in.

Oh, gods.

I caught up to him, wondering what to say, how to beg so he wouldn't run to King Maximus to claim his reward.

"Is it for you?" he asked without looking at me.

"Is what for me?" I said in a small croak that probably gave me away.

"Mr. Oakes sells bloodshade to me, too," he said. "Has for a long time."

My heartbeat echoed in my ears. Nyro was a Trove?

"It's not for me," he said as if guessing my question. "It's for… someone important to me."

Why was he telling me this? It was probably a lie to get me to admit I was a Trove.

"I still don't know what you're talking about," I said. "I was there to purchase something else." I thought of mentioning the smartweed, but I couldn't bring myself to do it, so I just added, "Something personal."

He stopped and faced me. When I continued on, he put a hand on my arm to stop me. My eyes darted to his fingers, then back up to his eyes, sending a silent "*take your hands off me*" message.

He kept his hand right in place. His dark gaze locked on mine. "Why did you become a Challenger?"

"Why did you? I didn't think they accepted thieves."

He sighed and removed his hand from my arm, clearly aggravated. "You need to stop calling me that. I told you my name."

"Nyro, I know." I don't know what made me acknowledge the fact, but it felt important.

He blinked, lips parting. "You remember."

I nodded. For a brief instant, he had been part of that world I'd left behind, a life in which strolling down the market with Talyssa was fun and easy, and buying pretty flowers for a vase was the most important event of the day.

"You were so beautiful that day," he said, surprising me. "Red looks good on you. I knew you were watching me."

His hand reached for mine, and I was too stunned to pull away. A thrill ran up my arm as his thumb caressed the top of my fingers. Something stirred in my middle, a wild restlessness I'd never felt.

"I couldn't believe you'd noticed me," he continued. "The gorgeous girl in the red dress, her skin like honey, her eyes near onyx. I wanted to talk to you, but..." he took a step closer, "I knew it wasn't my place. You, a lady, and me..."

He licked his lips. I swallowed, hypnotized by his intense gaze and velvet-soft voice.

"And now... enemies," he said, breaking me out of the spell. He let go of my hand, and I clenched it into a fist.

"I can't imagine what caused you to join the White Queen," he said, "but I know it must be hard for you. It's not the life for a lady."

"I... thank you for your concern," I said, sounding stiffer than I intended. "But I'm doing just fine."

"I can see that." Nyro nodded. "I'm glad. But be careful... with the bloodshade."

I was opening my mouth to say something, when I noticed movement out of the corner of my eye. With a jerk, I glanced down the road and saw Vinna and Alben a few yards away, staring in our direction.

"Um, I should go," I said, turning and taking a few steps away from Nyro.

"Wait," he said.

I glanced over my shoulder.

"Tell me your name." There was a certain longing in his face, as if my name would give him a key to something that should forever be kept out of his reach.

"Bianca," I said.

He nodded, satisfied. "I hope to see you again, Bianca."

"Me, too." I'd barely finished saying the words when—like a child who has done something wrong—I turned and ran toward Vinna and Alben.

"Was that a Blackie you were talking to?" Vinna asked, her voice a drunken slur.

"It was," I said. "I know him, from before."

"Well, that's unfortunate," she added, rubbing her face and swaying to one side.

"Yes, it is," I said. "Let's go." I slipped Vinna's arm over my shoulder, turning her in the direction of the White Palace. "It's late, and you're drunk."

"Where'd he go?" Alben said, blinking into the night.

I followed his gaze to where Nyro had been standing. He was gone.

"One minute he was there, and the next, *puff*," Alben said, following us with heavy, staggering steps.

"He tends to do that," I said, as we made our way back to our regimented lives.

14

The last few weeks of my training flew by. I wanted more time to prepare for this, but eight weeks was all they allowed. The contract even stated this date as the date my challenge should take place, if possible.

The other Challenger ahead of me, Miron, had come and gone, easily defeated by Skender. Not surprisingly, Mr. Piggy Eyes hadn't pardoned him. He'd been sent to Queen Lovina to become another meal, which gave me a clear image of my fate if I didn't defeat the bully today.

I very much doubted he would pardon me, even though I hadn't said anything about his relationship with Breen. But that was inconsequential, I had to win. I'd even laid out the ground work for my next challenge with Alben as a way to assure myself that I would beat Skender.

Sweat trickled down my back in an unladylike manner. I'd only just changed, and my shirt was already soaked. I slipped on my jacket, making the nervous sweat that had assaulted me even worse.

"It's time," Vinna announced.

I followed her out of the dormitory, and we walked toward the Challenge Hall. When we arrived, all the Pawns and Challengers were already there, including Skender.

"Good luck," Vinna whispered with a pat on my shoulder.

Alben gave me a thumbs up. "I hope yeh win."

I nodded. I had to win. My plan was in motion, but oh, gods, I didn't feel ready for this!

Swallowing the tight lump in my throat, I walked toward the center of the painted chessboard. I stopped in front of the pedestal that held the Challenge Vessel—I'd learned its official name since last time—and stood across from Skender. He wore a satisfied smile that was clearly meant to be a threat.

After merely a beat had passed, he quickly proceeded to stick his hand inside the vase. I didn't mind his haste, however. The suspense was terrible. I'd been on pins and needles for the last week, and I was ready to conclude this ordeal. If I ended up being the main dish at dinner time tonight, so be it. The Queen would drain me, and she would never discover I was a Trove because of the bloodshade in my veins.

Skender pulled out his hand, bringing the small, receptacle box out with him. Still holding the same smile, he handed it to me.

Please don't be a Knight. Don't be a Knight.

That was all I asked, all I'd been praying for since I learned what type of challenge drawing a Knight piece would entail.

With a deep breath, I opened the box.

The piece was, indeed, a Knight. I was as good as dead.

15

I looked at the stubborn mare in the eye.

"You *have* to listen today. You can't stop to eat weeds. My life depends on it."

The horse snorted as if to let me know what she thought of my pathetic life. Honestly, the mare had a better life than me. It had a roof over its head, food, someone—namely me—to clean after her. I even had to brush her mane and stinky tail every day.

"If I die, there'll be no one to clean up after you," I said, as if the beast could understand, as if it were true.

I sent a worried glance in Vinna's direction. She nodded and smiled in encouragement.

The sky was as blue as the irises Talyssa and I had planted early this summer, and not a cloud marred its beauty.

Not a bad day to die, I thought.

"What are you waiting for?" Skender leered at me from atop his horse. His bristly hair was standing on end as stiff as brambles.

With a sigh, I climbed my horse and pulled on the reins. The creature was nipping at a tiny patch of grass on the ground and took her sweet time to rear her ugly head and go to the start line, where Skender already waited, the satisfaction in his eyes as sickening as horse dung.

Breen, the First Pawn in our Quadrant and Skender's illicit girlfriend, stood next to the start line, holding a checked flag. We were on the oval track, where we rode each morning.

"Ready?" she asked.

Skender nodded. I did the same even though I felt anything but ready. We only had to race for one lap, but it might as well have been miles and miles for all the good my horse would do.

Breen pointed the flag toward the blue sky, then cried out, "Semper Lumen." The flag fell to the ground as she let it go.

Skender's horse leapt as he viciously struck its rump with the crop, then took off at a full gallop.

"I'm sorry," I mumbled and, also, struck my horse in the rear.

The beast let out a loud *neigh* and, for once, did as she was supposed to. Still, Skender had gained the advantage and was quickly turning the first bend.

"Beat him, please!" I pleaded with my horse. "You can do it."

To my utter surprise, the mare sped up, gaining enough on Skender that I could have reached out and touched him. Just then, he glanced under his arm and spotted me. His eyes widened, looking as if they might pop out and roll onto the track.

With a growl, he raised his crop and struck his horse harder than before. The animal cried out and lurched forward, kicking up dust into my face. I coughed, my throat clogged with dirt.

Wincing, I raised my own crop, but I couldn't bring myself to strike the animal again. If, to win, I had to hit the mare as hard as Skender had hit his mount, then I would lose. I couldn't be that cruel, no matter how many headaches the animal caused me. No one deserved to be mistreated that way.

So instead, I pressed closer to her, leaning forward and patting her neck.

"Good job so far," I said. "But I need you to try harder. Do you think you can do that?"

Of course, the mare didn't try harder. Instead, she started to slow down.

"No!" I screamed. "Go faster, faster!" I kicked my heels into her sides. "C'mon, girl. You can do this."

At this, the horse snorted and picked up her pace.

"Yes! That's it. Faster, faster, girl," I said.

Her legs pumped, hooves tearing the ground. The wind hit my face, sending wisps of hair in all directions. Heat and energy shot into my veins, and I started to feel as if I were flying.

Soon, we approached Skender on his right and caught up with him. For a moment, we galloped head to head, then started to turn the last bend. White uniforms waited at the finish line.

Skender beat his mount mercilessly, one strike after the next. The horse gained additional speed, trying to run away from the monster that kept tearing at its hind quarters.

"C'mon, c'mon, girl. You can do this," I encouraged my horse.

She sped up, and as impossible as it seemed, we got a nose ahead of Skender.

"Good girl," I said, patting my horse's neck. It was slick with sweat, and her breaths came hard and ragged.

Hooves beat the ground like thunder. Then, Skender caught up to us again, making me realize we were going to lose. He had the better horse. Mine was tiring already, unaccustomed as she was to doing more than snacking on weeds.

But it seemed the mere possibility of winning wasn't enough for my opponent, and to make sure of our loss, he switched the crop to his right hand and violently swung it at my horse's face.

With a cry of pain, the mare careened to the side and collided with Skender's mount. I cried out in turn as my leg was caught between the two animals. Skender's horse lost its footing and, tripping on its own legs, fell with a crash of bones and wild shrieks of pain.

As if he weighed no more than a feather, Skender flew off his horse.

A prayer caught in my throat. I hugged my mare's neck and shut my eyes, waiting to be thrown off or crushed under the weight of the animal. Neither came. Instead, my mount slowed down and, finally, came to a stop.

I sat there, pressed to her slick body, for what felt like an eternity. At last, I opened my eyes and sat straight, glancing around. Skender and his horse were on the ground—the animal's legs twitching, while Skender lay immobile.

Trembling, I dismounted and limped toward my opponent.

"Skender," I croaked.

He didn't respond.

A moment later, I reached him, then turned away with a gasp of horror. His neck was bent at an odd angle, and his eyes stared blankly toward the blue sky, reminding me of Papa, and the way his vacant gaze had been lost to the nothingness of a world beyond, a place where I could not reach him.

16

I limped back to my horse. She spooked a bit and tried to get away.

"Shh, it's all right," I said in a soothing tone as I took hold of her reins.

Angling her long face in my direction, I inspected the damage Skender's strike had caused. Blood seeped from a large cut above her eye. The eyelid was shut, covered in crimson and already swollen.

"Oh, gods," I said, the sight turning my stomach.

Would the poor animal lose her eye? I caressed the side of her face and spoke sweet nothings as I hugged her neck.

Rushing steps pulled me out of my despairing thoughts. I glanced up to find all the Pawns rushing in our direction.

Vinna arrived first, panting and looking almost as spooked as I felt.

"Are yeh all right?" She looked truly concerned. It warmed my heart and made me feel less lonely to have someone worry for my safety.

"I'm fine. My leg is a little bruised. That's all."

"Gods damn," Breen exclaimed, her gaze fixed on the fallen horse, ignoring Skender. "We'll have to put the beast down," she said, never glancing at her lover. After a long moment, she snapped out of it and whirled to face me. "What exactly happened?" she demanded, accusation in her expression.

Did she think I'd caused this? Would they take me away like they did Costin, assuming I dishonored the contract? I stared blankly at the ground, struck mute by fear.

"Bianca," Vinna said, taking my hand. "What happened?"

"We saw your horse crash against Skender's," Breen said between clenched teeth. "What did you do?" There was accusation in her tone. It seemed she'd already judged me and found me guilty.

"I…" My voice trembled. My leg throbbed with each of my frantic heartbeats. "Skender hit my horse with his crop," I finally managed. "She spooked and went wild. That's when we crashed into him. It all happened so quickly."

Breen just stared blankly. Alben walked up to my horse and checked her face.

"Holy Gambit," he cursed. "Poor beast."

"Let me look," Breen demanded, harshly yanking my mare's reins.

"Hey!" I exclaimed. "Treat her gently."

Vinna gave me a sideways glance and halfway smiled. I ignored her.

I took the reins from Breen and said, "She needs someone to check her injury."

"I'll take her," Alben said and, with an easy touch, pulled her away and walked her toward the stable.

"We need to take this to Knight Kelsus," Breen said, stomping after Alben and leaving us all behind.

17

Two hours later, I was lying down in the dormitory, trying to ignore the pain in my leg when Vinna came running in. She skidded to a stop at the foot of my flimsy cot and fought to catch her breath.

"What is it?" I sat up, my heart thumping.

Had my horse lost her eye? Or worse, had they put her down? They couldn't have. I hadn't even named her.

"Is the beast all right?" I asked in a low croak.

"What?" Vinna said, staring at me as if I'd gone crazy. "The horse? Now you care about it?"

I shrugged in answer, the same way she often did.

"No," she said. "'Tis nothing to do with the beast, Bianca. This is worse. Much worse."

"Oh, no." I put a hand on my chest as my heart sank.

They'd decided I had cheated, and tonight I would serve as Queen Lovina's dinner. I went cold as my eyes desperately roved around, looking for an escape, though I knew there was none.

"Breen's right mad," Vinna said. "Knight Kelsus listened to everyone's account of what happened, and he decided yeh won fair and square."

"He did?" I blinked, hardly believing what I was hearing. "So I won," I added—half question, half statement.

But if I'd won, why was Vinna staring at me with that strange look in her green eyes?

"Yes, yeh won," Vinna said as if that didn't matter. "Just the reason Breen lost it and went to Alben with a threat. I was looking after yehr horse in the stall, so she didn't know I was there. She told Alben if he doesn't get you to challenge him right away, she'll make sure to start a rumor."

"A rumor?" I threw my legs off the bed and stood up. "What rumor?"

"She said she's goin' start tellin' everyone that Alben's little sister's a Trove."

My spine turned to ice. "She's a... Trove?"

"No, yeh zugzwang." Vinna wrinkled her nose. "Of course she ain't a Trove. She's just a normal little girl. But that won't matter. They'll go for her, take her to the Queen to check. And once she's there," Vinna pointed in the direction of where the palace stood, "it won't matter that she ain't a Trove. The Queen will just..." She turned, grabbing her head in desperation.

"Breen has it in for yeh," Vinna continued. "She knows yeh're injured, knows yeh're in no shape for a challenge." She turned back and faced me. "She wants yeh dead, Bianca."

I collapsed back on the bed and buried my face in my hands.

Alben.

I thought of his jovial smile and easy way. Even though I'd known it would come to this, I still didn't want to fight him, didn't want to go through with this.

My leg smarted then, making me more aware of my injury. Even with my leg as it was, maybe I could still fight, maybe we could still…

And what if I managed to win convincingly? Would Breen still risk an innocent girl's life to get her way?

One way or another, I still had to fight Alben, and that meant today I would either become a White Pawn, or I would die.